My Sister's
Blue Eyes

My Sister's Blue Eyes

by Jacques Poulin

Translated by Sheila Fischman

Cormorant Books

Canada Council **Conseil des Arts**
for the Arts **du Canada**

ONTARIO ARTS COUNCIL
CONSEIL DES ARTS DE L'ONTARIO

The publisher gratefully acknowledges the support of the
Canada Council for the Arts and the Ontario Arts Council
for its publishing program. We acknowledge the financial support
of the Government of Canada through the Book Publishing
Industry Development Program (BPIDP) for our publishing activities.

Printed and bound in Canada

LIBRARY AND ARCHIVES CANADA CATALOGUING IN PUBLICATION

Poulin, Jacques, 1937–

[Yeux bleus de Mistassini. English]
My sister's blue eyes / Jacques Poulin; translated by Sheila Fischman.
Translation of: Les yeux bleus de Mistassini.

ISBN: 978-1-897151-05-1

I. Fischman, Sheila II.Title.
III. Title: Yeux bleus de Mistassini. English.

PS8531.082Y4813 2007   C843'.54   C2007-900422-9

Cover and text design: Tannice Goddard/Soul Oasis Networking
Cover image: istockphoto Inc.
Printer: Marquis Book Printing Inc.

CORMORANT BOOKS INC.
215 SPADINA AVENUE, STUDIO 230, TORONTO, ON CANADA M5T 2C7
www.cormorantbooks.com

Why do you crowd the world?

— EPICTETUS

1

The Murmur of Books

That morning, patches of fog had swept into rue Saint-Jean. With windbreaker collar pulled up and shoulders hunched, I was walking down the right-hand sidewalk, on my way out of Vieux-Québec. Suddenly, as I was going past the window of a bookstore, a burst of light caught my attention.

I stopped in my tracks.

A book was leaning against the back of the window. Its slate-blue cover showed a marine landscape illuminated by a lighthouse. At least that's what I made out at first glance, but a closer look showed me that the lighthouse was actually a stack of books topped by a lighted lantern. The title of the blue book was *A History of Reading*.

This beacon that I'd noticed, even so briefly — I myself was half lost in the fog — struck me a sign of fate. And so I went inside.

I hadn't been in this bookstore for a while. Everything had changed. There were still three steps to climb but after that, the first thing I saw, in the middle of the store, was a woodstove surrounded by wooden chairs and armchairs. The stove had stubby legs and a round belly.

I could hear murmuring, as if a number of people were conversing in an undertone, yet the store was deserted. Close to the door there was a counter with an old-fashioned cash register. Some distance away there was a desk with drawers and a reclining chair. At the very back I spotted a door that was slightly ajar: perhaps the murmur was coming from there.

Faking a cough to announce my presence, I went up to look at the books. I was in unknown territory: there were no bestsellers near the door or next to the cash register or on the low tables set out around the stove. The books that *were* visible I wasn't familiar with. And when I approached the shelves that covered the walls I couldn't figure out in what order the books were arranged.

A sad-eyed individual with grey hair and beard appeared in the half-open doorway at the back. For one brief moment I thought I saw my father, the year when he wasn't well and we'd rented a cottage that had drifted away.

"Greetings!" said the old man.

"Greetings," I replied.

"Are you looking for any book in particular?"

"Yes. The blue book in the window."

The old man seemed lost. Very quickly he pulled himself together and, going directly to a shelf on the opposite wall, he took down the blue book and handed it to me. The name of the author was Alberto Manguel. To make a good impression I adopted the tone of a connaisseur.

"What principle do you follow for shelving your books?" I asked.

"The principle of absolute disorder," he said.

For a moment I thought that he was pulling my leg or that he wanted to put me in my place. I was mistaken: his expression was candid and direct. He suggested I sit down to leaf through Manguel's book. While I was reading the first page and the table of contents, he picked up a few sticks of wood and some crumpled newspaper and lit a fire in the stove. Surprised at being the object of all this consideration, I looked at him more closely. It was then that I realized his face was familiar. He was Jack Waterman, the writer. He wasn't my favourite author, I'd only read his latest book quite recently, but his photo had been in the newspaper, book section. He was definitely older than the photo and he had eyes like a spaniel's. Ill at ease, I pretended that I didn't recognize him.

"May I ask a stupid question?" I inquired.

"Of course," he said.

"On my way in I heard a kind of murmur..."

"You did?"

"It seemed to be coming from the room at the back. Was it a radio?"

"Not at all."

After checking that the fire had taken, he closed the draft partially. He turned towards me and inspected me with curiosity.

"Did you really hear the murmur?"

"Yes."

"In broad daylight! Usually you can only hear it at night and even then you have to be very careful ... How old are you?"

"Twenty-five."

"That means that you have a gift!"

I could sense admiration in his voice and that was music to my ears; however, he hadn't answered my question.

"Where exactly does the murmur come from?"

"Oh, it's something quite well-known in bookstore circles," he said. "You place books of poetry here and there on the shelves, among the other books. As you know, poets are the guardians of the oral tradition and therefore they're always ready to recite their work. At night then, if you can't sleep and you're pacing the silent bookstore, you can hear the murmur of their voices and it's comforting."

I must have had my mouth wide open like a zouave, because he started laughing softly, then asked, "What do you do?"

"Nothing," I said. "I've just finished university and I'm looking for work. My name is Jimmy."

"What did you study?"

"French and English literature. The problem is, I don't want to teach."

"I need a clerk. Interested?"

"Maybe!"

My first impulse had been to answer: *Yes I'm interested! Right away if you want! The salary doesn't matter.* But some instinct always urges me to hide my feelings and to lie; I'm a despicable little rat.

He explained briefly that he needed help because now that his new novel had come out, he wanted to devote more time to a trade that he plied regularly: doing translations for Laval University.

"Where do you live?" he asked.

"In Limoilou, with my little sister. She's not around just now. She's often away."

"I know. It's the same for me with Gabrielle."

At that moment, I didn't pay close attention to what he was saying, because he was beckoning me to follow him into the back room. It was very small and he called it the Parenthesis: you could take four steps in one direction and five in the other. All the same, it had everything needed for eating and sleeping, including an ingenious system of collapsible, foldaway bunk beds.

"I sometimes sleep here," he said. "Shall I make way for you?"

"Okay!" I said.

"It isn't luxurious, but you know, Epictetus had even less: his sole possessions were a straw-filled mattress and a mat."

2

Rossignols, Best Sellers, and Manuscripts

The bookstore in Vieux-Québec was rather disconcerting.

One found there both trash and bestsellers, as in every bookstore, but their positions were reversed. Because he didn't like bestsellers, Mr. Waterman perched them on the highest shelves, in the place of unsold copies which are known in the profession as *rossignols*, and those books he placed prominently on the counter. He said that in nature, rather than perching on "the highest branches" of trees, real nightingales were in the habit of settling in the bushes at ground level.

Although spring had arrived, the air was still cool and damp, and the heat of the stove drew people inside. Customers, idlers, or simply people who liked coffee — all visitors were greeted kindly. Despite its modest size, the stove spread its warmth through the whole room, thanks to its angled pipe that ran the length of the ceiling, from which it was suspended here and there by metal pipe-collars. Firewood was kept in a tin box behind the counter.

The idea of putting in a stove was one that old Jack had taken from *A Moveable Feast.* He had been charmed by the passage in which Hemingway recounted his first visit to the bookstore Shakespeare and Company: when he pushed open the door, the writer, who was in his twenties at the time, had been greeted by warmth that came from the books piled up to the ceiling, from the stove that purred in the centre of the room, and from the kindness of the owner, Sylvia Beach, who had given him credit even though she didn't know him.

Jack Waterman hated stars, especially those in the small world of writers, and no doubt word had got around, because most of the people who came to sit around the stove didn't move in those circles. You might see, for example, a cashier from the Richelieu super-market, the owner of a Tourist Room on rue Sainte-Ursule, a nurse from the Hôtel-Dieu, a calèche driver, a journalist from *Le Soleil.* The presence of these people, and of many others, reminded Jack of parties he'd attended in his youth, at his father's general store, when regular customers, colourful characters who liked to talk, would get together and tell stories about fishing, hunting, and smuggling, while they smoked their pipes or took turns chewing and spitting tobacco, with varying accuracy, into the spittoon in the centre of the group.

Sometimes people brought us manuscripts. Generally they'd been turned down by publishers; sometimes it was the author himself, who didn't expect wide distribution and simply asked us to shelve the manuscript with the other books. One way or another, all these individuals were fragile and had to be treated like children, or almost.

During my first week on the job, I had the chance to meet the authors of several manuscripts. One was a young employee of the

Banque Nationale branch at the corner of Saint-Jean and de la Fabrique. He came on Friday, just before closing and, when I told him that Jack was away but that he always came to help me balance the cash, he decided to wait. He took a seat near the stove, holding a briefcase on his knees. I served him tea and fed the stove a small piece of maple just for him. His face was thin, his appearance somber as he sat on the edge of his chair and apologized for disturbing me. He made me think of Kafka, who was always apologizing too, in the *Letters to Milena*, which Jack had recommended I read.

Another day, a woman came in who had very beautiful green eyes in a face lined with wrinkles. She was holding a notebook, and from the way she pressed it against her heart with her two hands gnarled from arthritis, anyone, even a neophyte like me, would know that it was a manuscript. Actually, I was not surprised to see her because for some years now the number of old people in the population had been growing, and some of them felt that they were being helpful to their fellow-citizens by telling the stories of their lives. I suggested that she choose a place on a shelf for her manuscript herself, and after she'd walked around the room, with her head to one side so she could read the titles, she put it next to a novel by Anne Hébert.

One morning when I was unlocking the door, I found a young person sitting on a step outside. Despite the waves of blonde hair that masked the person's face and tumbled down to the collar of a suede jacket, I could tell that it was a teenage girl because of her delicate hands, which were spread over her manuscript. She was shivering. I showed her in and quickly lit a fire in the stove. I tried to warm her heart and all the rest, but like many people her age she was hermetically closed inside herself like a deep-sea diver in diving gear. I wished that my little sister were with me to give me a hand.

3

Eisenhower's Disease

Every night Jack came to give me a hand with the day's bookkeeping. He had explained everything when I arrived and I'd understood right away, but he felt the need to repeat his explanations, so I let him go ahead.

Under its quaint appearance, the cash register was outfitted with an odd computer system. Whenever a book was sold, the computer contacted the author: if he or she lived in the neighbourhood, he would run over and tail the buyer, note their address and try to find out what they thought of the book.

Once the day was over, I walked Jack to his place on rue des Remparts. It was a four-room apartment on the top floor, with a small terrace, planted with shrubs and flowers, that had a wonderful view of the marina, Île d'Orléans, and the splendor of the St. Lawrence. Sometimes he invited me for supper. I never knew in advance: he would decide at the last moment, after glancing at one of the windows in the apartment.

One night I saw that he was hesitating.

"Let's walk for a while," he suggested.

"All right," I said.

He led me towards the bottom of the street and began to talk about the time when he had lived in San Francisco. He told me he'd hung out at the City Lights Bookstore where he'd met Brautigan, Kerouac, and the great Jack London. That was impossible, he wasn't old enough, the dates didn't tally; his memory was playing tricks on him.

When he fell silent I changed the subject.

"How's your work going?" I asked.

"What?" he said.

"Your translation work..."

"I didn't work today... I had an appointment *there*."

We were behind the Hôtel-Dieu and he was pointing at the grey walls flanked by a tall chimney.

"An appointment with a gerontologist," he added.

"Are you sick?" I asked.

"Yes. I've got ... that disease ... what's it called? Ah, yes, Eisenhower's disease..."

At the last moment I refrained from telling him he was mistaken, that wasn't the correct name, because he was looking at the chimney very strangely: he was looking at it as if the smoke that it was belching towards the sky were extremely suspect. I chased from my mind some searing images in a documentary filmed in Germany at the end of the war.

"And?" I asked to restart the conversation.

"All is well. Apparently the disease hasn't progressed."

"That's good!"

"They ran half a dozen tests: intelligence, attention, concentration, judgement, songs..."

"Songs?"

"Yes, for memory. The gerontologist makes us sing songs that we like, and we'd better remember the words."

"Or else...?"

"Or else we're liable to get chips."

"To get *chips*?"

"Electronic chips! Microprocessors! Don't tell me you've never heard of them!" he exclaimed impatiently. "Some old people lose their memory completely, they don't even remember where they live! Doctors give them a bracelet or a chain with chips: that way there's always someone who knows where they are!"

Actually, I had read an article on the subject in *Le Soleil*. It even talked about hypodermic chips, implanted under the skin, but that wasn't common practice: it was an experiment conducted on some Texas prisoners on Death Row.

At the corner of the Côte du Palais, I nudged Jack slightly which made him turn left, away from that damn chimney. A little farther on I did it again, and this time he turned onto rue Charlevoix. That allowed me to lead him slowly home along the narrow streets of the Quartier Latin. I was concerned about what seemed to be going on in his head. As if to prove me wrong, he began calmly to sing a song that Catherine Sauvage had recorded, called "The Scarf."

If I wear at my throat
In memory of you
This silk souvenir
That remembers us two
It's not that it's cold
The day is quite mild

It's just that once more
Like a desolate child
I want to bring back
Your touch on my skin
Remembering all
That we once had been.

It was a difficult song, all in half-tones, that kept going up and down. He was a little off-key and started each phrase again at least three times, so that we'd arrived at his place before he had finished. He shook my hand.

"It's a song that Gabrielle is very fond of," he said.

4

Mistassini

One Saturday morning, I was standing with my elbows on the counter, reading. It was very early. I had just opened up and there weren't any customers yet.

It was early in May, the weather was milder, and the girls had taken off their tights and their salt-stained leather boots. I had started to read Epictetus, the Stoic, because I'd told Jack that I was familiar with him and I didn't want to be found out. After half an hour though, my mind was numb from the warmth of spring, and I set aside the philosopher to re-read one of my favourite books, *Treasure Island*, by Robert Louis Stevenson. I'd found it on the counter when I went to unlock the door: it was Jack, I assumed, who had taken it off the shelf for me.

The copy that he'd chosen was from the Bibliothèque Verte collection; it was illustrated with ink drawings and watercolours. I had been absorbed in it from the very first page when with renewed delight I saw the arrival at an inn on the seashore, on the road to Bristol, of "the brown old seaman with the sabre cut." He was square-shouldered and had "hands ragged and scarred, with black, broken nails; and the sabre cut across one cheek, a dirty, livid white."

My mind was wandering along the crest of an English cliff where "the surf roared along the cove and up the cliff" when all at once a dark shape that had come out of nowhere appeared across my path. For one brief moment I caught sight of an enormous feline with yellow bloodshot eyes that was threatening to pounce on me... Then I opened my eyes: on the counter in front of me was an ordinary black cat with a white spot under the chin.

At the same time, I sensed the presence of someone. I felt as if I were choking. A person had come in, no doubt at the same time as the black cat, and it wasn't Jack: he never arrived so early. Approaching me from behind just as I was about to turn around, the person's hands covered my eyes. Right away, from the softness of the skin, the curve of the fingers, from a hint of the scent of camomile that I'd known for so long, from the very slight breath that I could feel on my neck, and also from the beating of my heart, which was nearly out of control, I recognized my little sister.

She called herself Mistassini but that wasn't her real name. She'd chosen it because she adores the great rivers of the North and one of the times when she ran away she had worked on a wildlife preserve between Lac Saint-Jean and the Far North.

Most often I called her Mist.

"Hi, little sister! I didn't see you come in. I was lost in a story..."

"I could tell."

She wrapped her arms around my shoulders and pressed her cheek against mine. I put my hands over hers so that she couldn't move and so that I could feel the warmth of her chest on my back until the end of the world. On the counter the young cat, intrigued, stretched its neck towards me. I bowed my head and when my face was close to his, he rubbed his muzzle against my nose, which in the language of cats corresponds not to a greeting, as you might think, but rather to a question: "Friend or foe?" Apparently satisfied with the answer, he started walking up and down the counter, arching his back to brush against my chin and to walk over the book I was reading.

Mist had freed her arms. She was on my left, with her elbows on the counter too, and I kissed her on the ear. She had blonde hair cut very short. Her blue eyes were as luminous as ever. Mine were dark brown. She was light and I was shadow; sometimes I wondered if we had the same parents.

She must have gone first to our apartment in Limoilou, and probably it was the neighbour who'd told her where I was working. I never asked her any questions: she was free. She broke my heart, but she was free. We have no rights over the people we love.

"I'm very glad you're here," I said, with the sense that my words were inadequate for my feelings.

"Me too," she said.

"Is the little cat yours?"

"No, he was on the front steps when I arrived. I thought he lived here."

"No, not at all. I've never seen him before."

"Maybe he's hungry..."

"You're right."

I went to the Parenthesis and the black cat came out with a high-pitched meow and followed me, his thin spine rubbing against my legs. Mist came along too. She was lugging a big knapsack that I hadn't seen because she'd set it down on the other side of the counter when she came in. The cat devoured a piece of cooked ham and noisily lapped up two bowls of milk. After that, he walked around the room.

"He's glad to be here," Mist observed.

"You think so?"

"It's perfectly obvious."

"He can stay. It's his decision."

"It isn't big here but it's warm ... And over there, when you wake up at night can you see the stars?"

She was pointing at the skylight in the ceiling which Jack called "the light well."

"Of course," I said. "Except in winter, I imagine, because of the snow."

"But there's no bed?"

"There are two foldaway beds. I stow the mattresses behind the armoire."

I took a foam-rubber mattress from its hiding place and a pillow from the armoire. The mattress was in a floral cotton cover. I put it down on a scrap of carpet in front of the armoire, and Mist came over and sat on it with her legs crossed, after taking off her boots and socks and pulling up her skirt, which fell to her calves. The cat approached her, walked in circles for a few moments, then lay down between her heels and her stomach, as if that place had been reserved for him, and started to clean his muzzle and his whiskers.

My little sister had on a dark blue denim jacket and a skirt in the same fabric but paler, that had a slit in the front. Her tanned skin showed that she had spent the past weeks at other latitudes. I pretended I hadn't noticed.

"How about you, are you hungry?" I asked.

"No, but if there's any coffee..."

"Of course."

I put water to boil on the hotplate and poured three spoonfuls of coffee into the only remaining filter. When the water was ready, Mist got up from the bed and while I was pouring it over the coffee, she moved first one cup, then the other under the filter, alternating so that the two cups would be equally strong. Her hand didn't tremble at all, and mine only slightly.

She asked about my work and seemed very interested in all the details that put the bookstore in a class of its own. She seemed reluctant to believe me though when I told her that certain books were deliberately placed near the door so they were easier to steal, and that should it happen, Jack himself took care of paying royalties to the authors.

"But ... I noticed there's an anti-theft detector," she objected.

"It's disconnected," I said.

"Why not just give away the books to the customers?"

"We'd have tons of problems with the other bookstores. Already they give us dirty looks because we take in homeless people. They say it debases the profession."

I sat down beside her without spilling a drop. She asked another couple of questions, sipping her coffee, then her eyes began to shrink. The coffee warmed her so she set down her cup next to the bed and took off her jean jacket. Her head leaned towards me and slipped onto my thigh. Soon she was asleep and I didn't dare to move.

Girls always have a strange effect on me. Usually they appeal to me through a detail: a light in their eyes, a husky voice, a way of tipping their heads to one side. In the case of my little sister though, it's everything about her that's seductive.

5

Gravediggers

Apart from the moments when he lost his memory and those when he felt persecuted, Jack's behaviour was nearly normal and my sister and I enjoyed listening to him talk about the days when he was constantly on the road.

He had liked Mistassini from the outset. Before he even knew her plans, he'd offered her the hospitality of the bookstore and, if needed, his apartment. He was a generous, tolerant man.

Little by little, my sister ended up working regularly at the bookstore and a number of changes followed. As my work had been cut in half, Jack decided to initiate me into doing translations from English to French; he insisted that this profession had often brought in money when things were tight or when he was travelling.

I liked Jack's idea a lot; however, I hid my enthusiasm, my ideal being to seem detached from everything, like a genuine Stoic.

To stir my interest, he had made me a gift of his Powerbook, a somewhat outmoded portable computer that was good for word processing. He could afford this gift because, having done well in his annual examinations at the Hôtel-Dieu, he'd bought himself a Slow Writer Powerbook. As its name suggests, the swp was a model designed specially for authors whose output had been slowed down by age or by some other factor.

And so on days when Jack had trouble finding the words and spent a long time in the clouds, the contraption would wait patiently for him to get back to work, and if the old man took too long, it would encourage him in a mellifluous voice: "Don't worry, Mr. Waterman, the words are there, inside you. Take a deep breath."

Before supper, when we did the book-keeping, Jack would revise my translations and help me solve computer-related problems. Mist would join us, standing between and slightly behind us, and she would lean over my shoulder or Jack's, not missing a word that we said, and it was very pleasant to feel her breath on my neck.

One night, when Jack was trying to explain why English-speakers say *nager à travers la rivière* or *swim across the river* instead of *traverser la rivière à la nage* or *cross the river by swimming*, two young students came in. One of them stayed by the door while the other went to the counter and asked Jack for a package of airmail envelopes.

"I'm taking off now," he said, probably hoping for a smile from the girl. She was impervious to his word play so he turned around swiftly, just barely managing to keep his balance, and went to get the envelopes. We didn't sell stationery but he kept a supply of some items in the drawers of his desk to tide over customers. While he was busy looking, I noticed that the girl had positioned herself so we couldn't see her friend, who was still at the front door. Nonetheless, by craning my neck I was able to see the other girl just as she picked up one of the books stacked at the door and sped out. It was *L'Homme rapaillé*, the sole collection of Gaston Miron's poems.

After the other student had left I told Jack what I'd seen.

"Another Miron's gone," I told him.

"That's great!" he said. "Books are made to move around."

"Why do you do that?" asked Mist.

He thought for a moment.

"Because of the Diggers."

My sister and I exchanged a glance. We didn't recognize the name. I looked in my *Harrap's* and Mist came up with the translation at the same time I did: a *digger* was a *creuseur*. We were no further ahead. Then Jack cleared his throat and we could see that he had an irresistible urge to tell us a story. I switched off the computer. Mist was beside me and I could touch her elbow if I wanted. On the sidewalk across the street, the shadows were growing longer.

"In San Francisco during the sixties, there was a group of young people who were involved in street theatre," he began. "Their names were Ronnie Davis, Billy Landout, Peter Coyote, Peter Berg, Emmet Grogan... I'm sure I've left out someone."

"Weren't there any girls?" asked Mist.

"Sorry! ... Hang on now, the names are coming back. There was Suzanne Natural, Fyllis, Cindy Small, Bobsie ... All of them, boys and girls alike, put on shows in parks and other public places. They denounced political scandals, the power of money, traditional morality — all that. Do you understand?"

"Of course," I said. "Then what?"

"That was the time when San Francisco was taken over by a crowd of young people, many of them teenagers, who were flocking in from all over the United States and elsewhere. They were called 'hippies'. Does the name mean anything to you?"

We nodded in unison. As for me, I was wishing that he'd get to the point but evidently he had a weakness for the hippies and couldn't help telling us everything he knew about them.

"They were still kids," he said. "Kids with their heads full of dreams. They'd stuff a spare pair of jeans into a khaki bag they'd bought at an army surplus store, leave their wealthy parents' bungalows and, like Jack Kerouac, set out on the road to San Francisco. They would end up in Haight-Ashbury where the rents weren't too high. They dreamed of a world where everyone would live in brotherhood and peace, where each person would be free to broaden the field of his or her spiritual life with the help of drugs and psychedelic music, and the most naïve thought that to get there, all they had to do was let their hair grow, wear flowered clothes, and learn a couple of Allen Ginsberg's poems."

"Where do the Diggers fit in?" I asked.

Instead of answering, Jack said, "I like the hippies a lot, even if they were unrealistic. Dreams are very useful, in fact they're the best way to understand reality. And you mustn't forget that these young people who were leaving behind them the cold grey world of money were groping their way towards something more alive: adventure and human warmth. But I'm getting off the subject..."

"Not at all!" protested the biggest liar in Vieux-Québec.

"I'm glad to hear that! I'm getting to the Diggers... But wait, I remember some other names: Butler Brooks, Slim Minaux, and a girl, Nana Nina, and Richard Brautigan who turned up now and then... All of them, and the ones I named earlier, would get together in the evening, after the street theatre performances. They watched the hippies live, but with growing concern..."

"Why?" I asked, hoping to avoid a new digression.

"There were more and more of them in Haight-Ashbury and they needed help. They lacked money for a place to live or to eat properly, they suffered from diseases or bad trips, and the girls became pregnant. After thinking it over, the Diggers got the idea of providing them with one free meal per day. It was Emmett Grogan and his friends who took it on. They bought a used truck and started going to the central market in the suburbs early in the morning to stock up on — or steal if necessary — whatever fresh vegetables and meat people were willing to give them. Then they came back to town and turned the food over to their girlfriends who would cook it, generally making some kind of stew."

I rested my elbow against Mist's, because I'd just remembered the aroma of a chicken stew that my mother used to serve on Sunday night, with mashed potatoes. It was late and I was getting hungry.

Old Jack went on.

"The Diggers would come back in the afternoon. They'd pour the stew into big milk cans on the truck's platform and on the stroke of four o'clock, they would set up shop on the edge of Golden Gate Park, ready to serve a free meal to some two hundred starving hippies who'd bring a bowl and spoon and wait impatiently for this moment, having been informed by a leaflet that gave the time and place as well as the declaration: 'THIS IS FREE BECAUSE IT BELONGS TO YOU!'"

It was obvious that the remark was important to Jack because he repeated it twice, emphatically. Then he said, "For the Diggers, things belonged to those who needed them and not to those who had money. They felt that money, the race for profit, and private property were factors of social injustice. That was why in addition to the daily meal, they opened a store where people could pick up free clothes, a fridge, or whatever..."

"Used clothes and furniture?" asked Mist.

"No. Everything was new, aside from a few articles of cloth-ing that were placed outside the store to mislead the municipal authorities. And all those initiatives, including opening a free medical clinic and renovating a small hotel where runaways could stay — all that was done in total anonymity. The person in charge didn't come forward, no one claimed ownership of any business, there were no stars, no one gave interviews or signed their real names on official documents. And if someone turned up at the store and asked to see the person in charge, he was told: 'You want to see the person in charge? Look in the mirror: the person in charge is you!'"

"I'm starting to like these Diggers!" said Mist.

The light had nearly gone from rue Saint-Jean and it seemed to have settled on my little sister's face, especially in her eyes. Jack had stopped talking and like me, he was admiring the show.

Meanwhile, the black cat, who'd been christened Charabia because he possessed a bigger repertoire of meows than the average cat, jumped onto the counter and informed us in a plaintive tone that the time had come to serve him his meal. Mist murmured something in his ear, then she told Jack that there were two things she liked: the idea of stealing from the rich to give to the poor, and the decision to provide services to the community anonymously.

"Where did the name Diggers come from, though?" she asked.

"Actually," said Jack, "it was the name of a group of agrarian rebels who lived in Surrey, England, in the mid-seventeenth century. Because food cost too much, they took over some common land and distributed part of their income to their needy neighbours. The authorities saw them as troublemakers, anarchists like Robin Hood in the Middle Ages..."

He broke off. He seemed tired from the efforts he'd been making to remember some names and dates that were lost in his hazy memory. The circles under his eyes had got bigger.

"They were obliged to fight Cromwell's soldiers," he added in a weary voice. "Apparently they were given the name *Diggers* because they could often be seen digging graves at dawn to bury members of the group who'd been killed during the night."

And that was the end of the story. Obviously the final image had made a powerful impression on my little sister, because the light that we'd seen on her face a little earlier, which had dazzled Jack and me, had gone out all at once. It was probably to be forgiven for it that he invited her to his place for supper.

The invitation was valid for me as well. And for Charabia.

6

Gabrielle and the Full Moon

Since old Jack had a weakness for Mist, invitations to supper at his place became more frequent. However, neither my sister nor I knew what to expect when we walked him home.

One night I was with him and just as I was about to go back to the bookstore and Mist, something strange happened. I was trying to think of what we could have for supper aside from the eternal pasta, since neither of us was any good in the kitchen. He looked up at the window and as usual I had my hand out to him when all at once a smile lit up his wrinkled face. A smile that resembled a child's.

"Look!" he said. "She's there!"

I nearly asked who he was talking about, but at the last moment I modified the question: "Where?"

"Where do you think? The little window on the right!"

He was pointing at a window on the top floor to the right of his terrace. I had never seen Jack go into that room. The window soaked up the quivering and slightly bluish light of the full moon which had just come up.

"You can see that the window's lit up, can't you?"

"Of course," said the despicable little rat.

"Gabrielle has come back from a trip. I can't go in now, she needs to rest. Do you mind if we walk a little while we wait?"

"Not at all!"

To tell the truth, I was worried about my sister. My fears were unjustified because she got along perfectly well without me. She believed in total freedom: she didn't want to have to let me know when she would be away and she preferred me not to tell her either. It was out of the question then to call and let her know that I'd be late... But I couldn't help myself, and in any event I was worried.

Jack and I had started up rue des Remparts. There were a good many strollers taking advantage of the mild evening and of the light shimmering on the St. Lawrence. Jack had on his tennis hat, pulled down to his eyebrows, and even though it was late, he had on sunglasses. He hid his eyes, like those of a battered dog, which made him look a little like Salman Rushdie. The two of us could walk along peacefully without being disturbed by overly kind people who thought they were obliged to say hello and ask if he was "working on something."

In Montmorency Park he rested his stomach against a concrete parapet that jutted out over the cliff. He leaned over the sheer drop, a faraway look in his eyes.

"She's just back from a trip out west," he said. "She got a telegram from Manitoba saying that her mother had just died. So she took the train out."

I didn't ask any questions. He told me that she'd spent her childhood out there. It was close to where the great plains covered with wheat and flooded with sunlight began; they were so vast that you couldn't cross them in a single day, and when the stems rippled in the wind you felt as if you were on the ocean in a swell that ran all the way to the horizon.

"Would you like to stop for a drink?" I asked suddenly.

"Gladly," he said.

He led me towards the Côte de la Montagne. The choice surprised me because during our strolls, wanting to be kind to his old legs, he avoided this difficult descent to the Lower Town. At least he was turning his back on the Hôtel-Dieu, whose grey walls and sputtering chimney filled him with horror too because of images he'd seen in the film *Night and Fog*.

In the middle of the hill, he turned right onto the big wooden staircase, and after the first flight of steps he stopped in front of a bistro. I followed him inside, where he settled at the bar, standing between two stools to spare his poor back.

The barmaid knew him. She came around the counter and embraced him warmly, rubbing his lower back. She was taller than he was and sturdily built, with broad shoulders and muscular arms. Jack introduced me as his associate in the bookstore, but I was only entitled to a handshake. She couldn't know that I had a recurring dream in which I was snuggled in the arms of the Norwegian javelin thrower Trine Hattestad, a superb athlete who was holding me tightly enough to crush me.

Jack ordered two kirs without asking what I wanted. While we waited for the drinks he went out on the terrace where there were a few tables, and from where I was at the bar I could see that he was looking up at the sky. The barmaid started to mix the cassis with the white wine in front of me. She jerked her head in his direction.

"How is he doing?"

I didn't know what to say.

"Are you asking because of the moon?"

"Of course. There's nearly always a full moon when he comes to see me. Did he talk about Gabrielle?"

"Yes, but just a few words," I said in a hushed voice.

"What do you think about it?"

"Nothing. I don't have the means to judge other people."

That was a remark I'd heard on some detective show or other on TV, but it won me a very sweet smile. The barmaid's cheeks were chubby and ruddy and she had on a sleeveless sweater that it was hard to take your eyes off.

"What are you looking at?" she asked.

"Your shoulders," I said, with the feeling I was sinking into a lie. "Are you a swimmer?"

"Yes. How can you tell?"

"Your shoulders are broad enough for two people!"

"Are you thinking about anyone in particular?"

This time her smile was teasing; I still found it irresistible because it was meant just for me. I hunted in vain for something nice to say. Fortunately, Jack came back from the terrace and we began to sip our drinks. Five minutes later he went out again to look at the moon.

"She's as beautiful as ever," he said when he came back, "but there must be clouds coming from the east, because I can't see any stars there."

He seemed serene, almost detached from reality. It was very pleasant to listen to him and the barmaid when they started to talk about literature. She was a very experienced reader of novels and she had a rare virtue: she could find a good many connections not only between the books of one author but also between those by different authors who at first glance had nothing in common. It was a virtue that Jack particularly appreciated, because he too had worked out a theory which maintained that works of literature were, contrary to appearances, the fruit of a collective effort.

Pursuing his analysis, he offered the suggestion that instead of repeating themselves or writing their memoirs, old writers would be wise to seek out young ones who would be able to take over. All at once he broke off, looked at the time, and gulped the rest of his kir.

"It's getting late," he said.

"You're right."

I downed my drink in turn. The barmaid kissed Jack on both cheeks and this time, she put her arms around me: it was a moment of happiness, I closed my eyes, imagining that Mist was with me and that she was sharing my pleasure.

The kir and the embraces emboldened us to go up the staircase and then the Côte de la Montagne. When we got to the steepest part Jack was breathing so hard that I decided to stop. I scrutinized the starry sky, claiming that I was trying to find Venus. He recommended that I look towards the west, above the former Grand Séminaire, but the sky was overcast and I couldn't see a thing. We resumed our climb in the company of a group of tourists coming back from an excursion to the Place Royale or to rue du Petit-Champlain.

When we were across from the apartment on rue des Remparts, the clouds had gained more ground. Only one thing though was of interest to Jack: the little window on the top floor.

"Ah! The light's off!" he said.

"You're right," I said, inspecting the window.

It was now as dark as the rest of the sky and the depths of my heart.

"Don't worry, it's a good sign."

"You think so?"

"Yes I do. It means that Gabrielle is resting. She travelled across Manitoba, Ontario, and part of Quebec. The train isn't fast, it's a long trip, and now she's sleeping."

"Of course."

"I'll go inside in a while. It's best to wait... You don't have to stay."

"I know."

"Look, I'm going to sit on the bench over there. I'll wait fifteen minutes, then I'll tiptoe inside."

Nearly opposite his place, on the right, was a small square at the edge of the cliff, with one park bench and a streetlamp. He sat down there and I did the same.

"I'll stay a while longer."

"Looks like rain," he said.

"Yes," I said looking at the sky which was getting darker and darker.

7

The Interview

I sensed it when I woke up that Sunday morning: something unusual was going on in the Parenthesis. It was cold and I got up reluctantly.

Mistassini wasn't there in the top bunk. In the bathroom, her toothbrush and her personal belongings had disappeared. Still half asleep, I put water on to heat and only then did I notice that her big knapsack wasn't there either. Nor was it in the big room. Once again, Mist had gone away and she had respected our agreement: no warning, no apologies, no goodbye.

I leafed through *The Handbook* of Epictetus, looking for a word of consolation. I could only find this phrase, underlined the first time I'd read it: "Do not ask things to happen as you wish, but wish them to happen as they do happen and your life will go smoothly."

The kettle had been whistling for a while now. After adding a little water I took from the fridge the litre of milk, the butter, and the bitter orange marmalade, and I put some rye bread in the toaster. I was sipping my coffee, pensive, when a noise from the entrance made my heart race. Someone was opening the door to the bookstore and at first I thought that Mist had changed her mind. I went on drinking my coffee as if nothing special were going on. Charabia was drinking his milk with his eyes half-closed and looking as innocent as I did.

The front door closed and unfortunately, instead of the furtive gliding of Mist's moccasins, I heard a two-note cough: it was Jack's way of announcing his presence when he didn't see anyone in the store. Why was he here on a Sunday morning? And why so early? True to my habit and to Stoic principles, I kept my questions to myself.

Jack was nervous and irritable. He realized that Mistassini wasn't there though he didn't notice that she'd taken her belongings. I fixed him a cup of hot chocolate which he took, saying that he was expecting a journalist. He settled in at his desk and stretched out in his reclining chair, feet propped on the edge of a partly open drawer. I sat in a corner with Charabia and Epictetus on my knees.

Three quarters of an hour later the journalist arrived. He was in his forties, wore thin wire-rimmed glasses, a burgundy leather jacket, and had a bag slung over his shoulder, from which a camera emerged.

"Sorry to be so late," he said, "I didn't hear the alarm. I went to bed at dawn because I was reading your book... In fact, I didn't have time to finish it."

Jack muttered something, assumed an indifferent manner, and took a long sip of hot chocolate. The journalist rummaged in his bag and took out a portable tape-recorder, which he set up on the desk. Even from a distance you could see the red light indicating that it was on. Jack got up slowly and without hesitating, switched off the device.

"That's the best model in the world!" the journalist protested. "A gem! You can talk for hours! You can pace while you're talking! It lets us have a normal conversation!"

"Put your gem back in your bag."

"Too bad! I can take notes but I'll be asking you to repeat yourself all the time, to be sure that I quote you accurately."

"Are you in the habit of quoting authors accurately?"

"No!"

The journalist stowed his tape-recorder, took out a notebook and pen. He started to laugh.

"I'm going to tell you a secret," he said. "Good journalists know that we must never quote faithfully the subject of an interview. If we did, they would hold it against us for the rest of their lives! Do you know why?"

Sitting in my corner I expected that Jack would reply: "No, but you're going to tell me!" or something like that. It was quite the opposite, he acted as if he hadn't heard. From a Stoic point of view, it was a respectable attitude. Not in the least discouraged, the journalist went on,

"Most authors can't speak very well. They'll start a sentence, stop to search for a word, lose the thread, and finally say something that's completely off the topic. When we quote them, we have to reconstruct what they wanted to say."

"I certainly feel sorry for you! Would you like a coffee?"

"Yes, please. Black."

Without waiting for Jack to ask me, I got up from my corner and went to the Parenthesis to make more coffee. While I was in there with Charabia, the journalist asked the traditional question.

"Why do you write? I know that's not very original..."

"To see my name in the paper and to get women interested in me," Jack replied.

"Does it work?"

"Not well enough. What about you?"

There was a silence. I stuck my head out the open door, thinking that the journalist was going to make Jack understand, by showing him an inscrutable face, that he was the one who'd ask the questions. On the contrary, he smiled. You could see that he was a kind and reasonable man. I brought him his coffee. He thanked me politely, took a sip, and turned to Jack.

"Where were you born?"

"I could tell you, but then you'd ask what my parents did, how many children they had, whether I had a happy childhood, and so on. So I'm telling you straightaway: my childhood is none of your business, that's my private life, it's the source of my writing and I don't share it with anyone! Clear enough?"

"Absolutely," said the journalist in an unflappable tone that contrasted with the forcefulness of Jack's remarks. "You'd rather we talk about your book?"

"You can always try..."

"Did it take you a long time to write it?"

"Four years."

"What about it was hard?"

"The words wouldn't come. Or rather, they came in dribs and drabs."

The journalist, who was noting Jack's replies, looked up from his notebook to see if the writer wanted to explain. Scratching the top of his head, where there was a kind of tonsure, Jack seemed to be thinking, but he refrained from commenting.

"Was it easier in the past?"

"Yes. In the past I was able to write one page a day, whereas now it's hard for me to do half a page."

"In how many hours?"

"Four or five. Maybe there's something abnormal going on in my head..."

"Or perhaps it's simply a matter of rhythm. Your rhythm is slower than average, that's all. To each his rhythm!"

"To each his rhythm," Jack repeated softly, as if he were weighing the expression to see if it applied to him. I had good reason to think that it didn't. One night he'd invited me to his place to watch a literary show on television where one of his colleagues, a very popular writer who brought out at least one book a year and who often appeared on TV, was going to take part. Questioned about how he worked, the colleague had said that he wrote fifteen pages or so every morning before breakfast, then went to the university where he taught full-time. When he added without boasting that he had in his drawers a detailed outline of his next three novels, Jack had flung one of his slippers at the screen, just missing his target but shattering a lamp that sat on top of it.

If I was the biggest liar in Vieux-Québec, Jack wasn't far behind me.

"Are you happy with your book?" asked the journalist.

"I'm happy that I've finished it," said Jack.

"You don't like it?"

"Unfortunately it's a long way from what I wanted to do. In the beginning I didn't know where I was going. That's normal. I groped my way for a year and then one night I had something like a flash of inspiration. I saw the direction my story was taking, I saw the role of each character, I even found the *tone* for the narration. After that I simply tried to avoid the pitfalls and get to the end of the road."

"Like a marathon-runner..."

"Except that I'm not a fast runner!"

They laughed for a moment and drained their cups. I went back to the Parenthesis to put more water on to boil. Charabia came with me and lapped up some milk. The journalist was the first to turn serious again.

"You talked about *tone*," he said. "Does that matter a lot?"

"Indeed it does."

"Is it different from what's known as *style*?"

"For me it's the same thing."

"Then what is style exactly?"

I pricked up my ear because of the hissing of the water as it heated up. Jack began to hesitate and his remarks became a little confused. I understood though that for him, style had nothing to do with the "beautiful writing," that reviewers often talked about: it was something more profound. He tried to clarify his thoughts, but I understood nothing of his explanations, except that style is a translation of the author's personality.

"Basically," the journalist summed up, "you're trying to say something very much like the old saying, 'The style is the man.'"

"No, I would say, 'The style is the soul,'" replied old Jack.

That trivial little statement seemed to disconcert the journalist: when I brought out fresh coffee and chocolate, I saw that he had his mouth open and his pen in the air. I though, even if I didn't know exactly what it meant, much preferred it to Jack's often excessive remarks on the subject; one day he'd told a literary critic that in a novel, style was the most important factor and that everything else depended on it: the choice of subject matter, the action, the characters and all the rest...

I went back to my corner and buried myself in Epictetus, while keeping an eye on Jack. The journalist started up again.

"While I was reading you I wondered why your protagonist was so passive..."

"That's a ridiculous word," said Jack.

"*Passive?*"

"No, *protagonist*! I know it's a fashionable word but when you say it I hear a little engine going *prrttt* and then I hear '*agony*'! It's hard not to laugh..."

"Do you prefer the word *character*?" asked the journalist calmly.

"Yes."

"So why is your character so passive?"

"Who knows? Don't take offence..."

Jack broke off and sipped his hot chocolate, gazing intently at the face of the journalist, who gave no sign of irritation and waited calmly for what would come next.

"I may as well tell you the whole truth," said Jack. "It's impossible for me to answer that kind of question. Most authors can. In fact they know everything. They know what's going on in the heads of their characters, and in their hearts and even in their unconscious. Lucky them! But I only see my characters from the outside. They look a little like me, but they're strangers; I don't know a thing about them... Say, that could be the title of your article: *The Man Who Knew Nothing.*"

"You have doubts about yourself, like all creative artists..."

"Novelists aren't creative artists! They take their inspiration from reality, they transform it, they add personal experiences, imagined experiences, even experiences that they've borrowed or stolen: a novel is actually a do-it-yourself project!"

"That depends on how it's done... According to the critics, your way of doing it is minimalist. Does that word still suit you?"

"Yes. I'm faithful to Raymond Carver's principles. Even though I try to vary the form of the sentences and make them flow more freely so that I won't bore the reader, I prefer to say things in the fewest words possible and to avoid beautiful images and clever turns of phrase."

"Besides Carver, who are your favourite authors?"

"Stevenson, Salinger, and most of all, Hemingway ... but actually I don't really like authors, I like books. A few books. Maybe a dozen. Brief stories told in a special tone. I don't like much, unfortunately. It's even possible that I don't like literature."

Jack's expression had become gloomy and I thought to myself that the journalist, busy taking notes, might not notice the change. I was wrong.

"And in life," he asked with a clear note of sympathy, "what matters for you?"

"Details," said Jack. "What shines in children's eyes... A cat cleaning his whiskers with his paw... The infinite play of light in the leaves of trees... The heart-rending lament of a Ferrari in the right lane of the stands at Monza..."

"What is the main virtue of a writer?"

"Foolhardiness."

"Why do you say that?"

"I have no idea."

The journalist wrote down the answers, then closed his notebook.

"That's it," he said. "I'll snap a few photos and I'm out of here. One last question, just between us: what would be a good book?"

"I already told one of your colleagues: a good book is one that makes you want to turn the pages to know how the story ends but you restrain yourself for fear of missing the virtues of the writing... Now, to thank you for patiently taking notes without complaining, I'm going to give you a brief text. It will entertain your readers."

"Wait! If I've taken notes here and there it was to put you off track. A while ago you turned off the tape recorder and told me to put it in my bag... I did, but when I was putting it away I turned it on and it's running at this very moment!"

"Good for you! Your skill is one more reason for me to make you a gift of this short text. I composed it from a model I found in a newspaper."

Laboriously, he got out of his reclining chair, then rummaged in a desk drawer, the middle one, took out this printed text, and read it aloud.

The Writer's Ten Commandments

1. You shall throw out your first novel.
2. You shall steal your colleagues' ideas.
3. You shall not answer critics.
4. You shall not go out for lunch with your publisher.
5. You shall refuse literary prizes unless they're accompanied by a sum of money.
6. You shall not check to see if your new book is in the stores.
7. You shall speak ill of your colleagues but only behind their backs.
8. You shall not write your memoirs.
9. You shall try to die young.
10. You shall not appear on TV.

8

The Little Push

Mist hadn't come back yet. Not wanting to leave me with all the work, Jack was coming to the bookstore more often. Despite the difference in age, we were becoming closer and closer.

The work had increased for a very simple reason: a sudden return of the cold had prompted us to light the stove again, and immediately our winter readers, lovers of coffee and small fires, had come back. They were quiet people, but among them were a few loudmouths over whom I had no authority. When they drank too much beer or cheap red wine, Jack would get up, grab the poker, and stir up the logs in the stove. After that, all he had to do to restore calm was to hold the reddened poker in his hand for a few seconds; he didn't even have to look at the troublemakers.

I had tried unsuccessfully to copy him.

During my free time he continued to teach me how to translate from English to French, using articles he himself was responsible for translating for the *Dictionary of Canadian Biography*. These articles, which recounted the life of a figure, often little-known, from Canadian history, presented no particular difficulties; it was a matter of achieving a text that was harmonious in French while staying as close as possible to the English. Yet once my work was done, when I compared my translation with Jack's I had to admit that I made a number of mistakes: inaccurate vocabulary, awkward turns of phrase, lack of restraint.

To add interest Jack would sometimes use literary texts that were available in both languages. In particular, he liked the short stories of Hemingway and Fitzgerald. One day, he showed me a Hemingway story entitled "The Battler," which began like this.

Nick stood up. He was all right. He looked up the track at the lights of the caboose going out of sight around the curve.

He asked me what I thought of the French version.

Nick se leva. Il n'était pas blessé. Il regarda la voie devant lui à la lumière du wagon de queue qui disparaissait dans une courbe.

According to my Harrap's, the equivalent for the word *caboose* was *fourgon de queue*, but that was the only error I could see.

"There are two mistakes," said Jack. "A small one you can't see and a big one that's staring you in the face."

"I'll look for the big one first."

Reading the rest of the story gave me a clearer idea of the situation Hemingway describes. His character, the young Nick, had hopped on a freight train without paying. Caught by the brakeman, he'd just been given a push that had thrown him off the moving train. After landing on his hands and knees beside the track, he stood and checked that he was all right while the train went out of sight around the curve. Then I wrote, *Nick se leva...*

"...*se releva*," Jack corrected. "That's the small mistake I mentioned."

"Thank you. *Nick se releva. Il n'avait rien. Il regarda, à l'autre but de la voie, les lumières du fourgon de queue disparaître dans un tournant.*"

"Not bad! I'd get rid of the commas so the sentence will reproduce the steady movement of the train. Okay?"

"Okay. "

"Then, for euphony, I'd say: 'Il *vit à* l'autre bout ... instead of *il regarda à* l'autre bout...' But you did pretty well! You deserve a good supper, my treat! "

I protested for form's sake, so happy to note that Jack had all his faculties. On the other hand, I was fairly pleased with myself and I was imagining the tender look that Mistassini would have given me if she'd been there. My progress however provoked some concern: I was becoming aware that the ties developing between words and me were liable to last a long time, maybe even take up too much room in my life.

When the customers and idlers had left the bookstore, Jack took me not to his place but onto rue Sainte-Angèle, to his favourite Italian restaurant. When the waitress saw him arrive, she disappeared into the kitchen and came back with an orange crate. She set it on a table in the corner next to the oak buffet and covered it with a small scalloped cloth. With that setup Jack could get into the most comfortable position for his lower back, i.e. half-sitting, half-standing, backside resting on the edge of the buffet, elbows on the orange crate. I had to raise my head to talk to him, but that was nothing new: he had the same kind of arrangement at his place on rue des Remparts, except that there he used a sturdy plastic crate instead of a wooden one.

While the waitress was getting menus, I asked Jack the question that was running through my mind.

"Do words put up a wall around you? Do they close you inside a tower?"

Instead of replying, he became absorbed in the menu. I wasn't even sure that he'd heard. The silence persisted. The waitress had come back and taken our orders. Only then did Jack reply.

"That's the wrong question."

"What do you mean?"

"The right question to ask is whether we choose life or a representation of life."

"So which one should we choose?"

"A representation of life is a thousand times more interesting. Except that near the end..."

He left the remark unfinished and a certain number of ghosts approached the table amid a threatening silence. I was relieved when he came back to more concrete matters.

"Any word from Mistassini?"

"To tell the truth I don't expect any."

"You don't think she'll come back?"

"She will, in her own time. We won't know in advance, just one fine day she'll be there."

"I miss her," he said.

"Me too," I said.

"And I miss Gabrielle."

He heaved a small sigh.

"Women are dreams," he concluded.

The waitress arrived with our food. She had heard Jack's last remark and as she set down his risotto milanese on the orange crate, she bestowed a resounding kiss on his forehead. He closed his eyes and let his grey head drop onto the girl's bosom. She said nothing, only waited, smiling. Jack was smiling too but he looked like an old child and the sight made me uncomfortable.

One thing I liked very much. When he talked about Mist he didn't say "your sister," which would have been a way of putting me in the wrong; he always used her name or her nickname. Another thing I liked: he had stated that in loving relations you're allowed to do whatever you want, as long as you don't impose your will on the other person.

"There's something I'd like to ask you," said Jack. "In fact it's the reason I invited you here."

"I thought it was because I'm making progress as a translator..."

"Sorry, I often forget things that have just happened. Luckily I still remember old things."

To reassure himself he started to hum "Marie-Hélène," one of Sylvain Lelièvre's oldest songs. He sang it all the way through, without a mistake as far as I could tell. People at nearby tables looked at us kindly, some even with a kind of complicity.

When the song was over, Jack withdrew into a silence that lasted till dessert. He was frowning, his face was agitated by nervous twitches. When she brought the fruit salad with ice cream that we'd ordered, the waitress whispered something in his ear. He took a flask from his pocket, dropped two tablets in his hand, and swallowed them with a little water.

All at once he seemed astonished to see me across from him, then he pulled himself together.

"What were we talking about?"

"You wanted to ask me something..."

"Right ... Again, I have to come up with the right words..."

He nibbled at his dessert, muttering something incomprehensible, moving his head first to one side, then the other, as if trying out different formulations. Then he sipped some hot chocolate and used his finger to wipe a little foam that had caught in his moustache.

"Here it is," he said. "It's about the disease I have, that I always forget the name of... I've talked about it before, remember?"

"I remember very well," I said, trying not to let my concern show.

"You see, that disease is ... pernicious. There's no cure; over time it will only get worse. All you can do is postpone the deadline. One day things get all tangled up and you don't really know who you are. It's like being lost. You can't manage on your own, you're like a child... So the question I want to ask you..."

He wasn't altogether ready. To give himself time to think, he asked the waitress for another scoop of ice cream in his fruit cup. He mixed the ice cream with a bit of hot chocolate and began to savour it very slowly.

"My question is this," he resumed. "On the day when I lose my faculties, I don't want to be shipped off to the Hôtel-Dieu and I don't want to be anyone's responsibility. For me, that will be the time to go. Only I don't know if I'll be able to do it myself so I may need a ... a little push. I want to know if you'd agree..."

I held my hand up to let him know that I understood and that he didn't have to say anything else. He added that I didn't have to give my answer then and there.

"I'll think about it," I said.

I was lying. I was actually doing a sordid calculation. Since he was losing his memory, old Jack would probably forget that he'd asked me the question: with a little luck I wouldn't have to reply.

I was ashamed of myself.

He asked if I'd enjoyed my meal and if I wanted anything else. I didn't. He pushed away his orange crate and left the restaurant without saying goodbye to the waitress or to the two or three people he knew. He forgot to pay, but the waitress let me know through gestures that it didn't matter, she would take care of it later.

I followed him onto the street and, so as not to leave him abruptly, I walked him home to rue des Remparts. I didn't say anything, I felt like an idiot because I hadn't had the courage to assume my responsibilities.

When I went back, rue Saint-Jean was nearly deserted because of the chill in the air, and way up above the stars struck me as cold and inaccessible. I had a hunch that Mist wouldn't have come back. I was not mistaken.

9

Conversation With the Publisher

Around five o'clock one afternoon, Jack phoned me. His publisher was coming over and he wanted me to be present at the interview. Mist still wasn't back so all I had to do was close the store after I'd shooed the customers away as gently as I could.

On rue des Remparts the stairs to Jack's place seemed to have been specially designed not to tire his legs. After the first rather steep steps you quickly came to a landing that opened onto a corridor which led towards the back, and from there, in small stages, you could climb effortlessly up to the top floor.

The apartment had four rooms that opened onto each other, the most pleasant being the living room in front, which had a magnificent view of the St. Lawrence. There were also a big kitchen, a library, and a bedroom with bathroom. In the kitchen, a French window and two cement steps led onto a small terrace planted with shrubs and flowers; on the other side of the terrace, if you climbed up two identical steps you gained access to an additional room that I'd never entered: the mysterious room whose window, one night when the moon was full, had been lit up by a fleeting glow.

When I got there, Jack and his publisher were having a drink on the terrace. Jack introduced me and made such laudatory remarks about my translation work that I didn't know where to look. Not only did he declare that I'd made spectacular progress, which was sheer exaggeration, but he also let it be known that I had literary ambitions which I hadn't yet admitted to myself!

They were on the part of the terrace that Jack called the solarium; it was a space sheltered from the wind and lined with young conifers, under the roof overhang. Stretched out comfortably on chaises longues, they were enjoying the first really mild spring day. The publisher, a tall, thin, distinguished-looking man, was barefoot and smiling with pleasure; I was impressed by his attentive and benevolent gaze. Jack had on just shorts and his tennis hat. His thinness was extreme and I who saw myself as broad-minded felt like a voyeur at the sight of his emaciated shoulders, his bony chest, his legs like stilts. Half-turning my back to him, I picked up a can of beer and sat in a garden chair across from the publisher.

"May I ask what you intend to write?" asked the publisher politely.

"I haven't the slightest idea!" I declared, rather pleased with this response which at least didn't contradict what Jack had been saying when I arrived.

"You've got all the time in the world..."

"People always say that."

The publisher's grin widened.

"In the meantime," he said, "you have to read a lot and you have to travel."

"That's what I think, too," said Jack.

"And what about you, Mr. Waterman, how are you?"

"I'm a walking wreck. Aside from that, everything's fine."

"Are you working on anything?"

"No."

"Maybe it's just as well."

I turned my head towards Jack, but since his tennis hat came down over his eyes and he'd put on sunglasses too, I couldn't tell if he was offended. I expected the worst, knowing his tendency to think that the whole world was lined up against him. What's more, when he was having an attack of paranoia, for some obscure reason his neurons jammed more easily and it wasn't long before you could see the effects of the disease that he couldn't remember the name of.

"Would you rather I didn't write?" asked Jack in a voice quivering with indignation.

"No, I just mean that it's good to have a break between books, take some time off for living. As Hemingway did. It's a way to invigorate the inspiration."

"Do you think that my books are too much alike?"

"Not at all, Mr. Waterman! Why do you ask?"

The publisher had straightened up in his chaise longue, setting his feet on the tiled floor. His surprise was genuine.

"Because it's exactly what I think: they're too much alike," Jack replied. "Something in my head's become unhinged."

"But if they were too much alike I wouldn't publish them!" the publisher added. "Besides, they wouldn't sell."

"Like the latest one?" asked Jack.

"On that you're mistaken: it's selling rather well, considering that you've only given one interview..."

Jack lit a cigarette. Of late he'd gone back to smoking, drinking, and eating whatever he felt like.

"Look," he said, "surely you don't want me to promote my books."

"Other writers do, or most of them!"

"They do it instead of you!"

"What do you mean?" asked the publisher calmly.

"In contracts you undertake to publish the books, distribute them, and *make them known*, don't you?"

"Something like that..."

"As for *making them known*, you don't fulfill your obligations very well. It's the author who gets stuck with all the work: newspapers, radio, TV... The person who's worn himself out to write the book, who's used up all his strength and all his talent, still has to make the rounds of the media and answer the same questions ten times. Aren't you ashamed of yourself?"

The publisher did not reply right away. No doubt he was hoping that Jack himself would realize on his own that he'd gone too far. I also thought his remarks were too extreme. Mist and I had already considered this question and we'd concluded that authors had nothing to complain about: no one forced them to write and if they thought that kind of work was too hard, they could always choose something else.

"Most authors are happy to answer journalists' questions," declared the publisher.

He was right. I myself had seen on TV authors smile with contentment that grew broader as the host listed their books.

"They're full of themselves," said Jack. "They say they've been given a mission, that they write almost in spite of themselves, as if someone were dictating the words to them, and that they feel an uncontrollable need to communicate."

"And that's not true?"

"The truth," he said with suppressed anger that was unusual for him, "is that the writer's work has nothing to do with communication. On the contrary, writing is a totally egocentric activity, and those who go in for it are only interested in themselves and in satisfying their own needs."

I settled into my garden chair, knees pulled up, face hidden by the can of beer that I was holding in both hands; I was waiting for the storm to blow over. The publisher didn't have the same reaction at all.

"You're right," he said, "we always write for ourselves. That's a truth we discover over time. But if some people think otherwise, why bother setting them straight?"

"It's pointless," Jack conceded in a tired voice.

He got up, stretched his legs, bending his back in every direction. The publisher got up too and so did I. The terrace encouraged peace and harmony, with its young trees growing in big tubs of earth and its flower baskets hanging from the posts that supported the overhang of the roof; it was like being in a garden. One night when the breeze from the St. Lawrence drove away the mosquitoes, Mist and I had been given permission to sleep there, wrapped in Jack's big sleeping bag, and we hadn't nodded off until dawn, after spending hours looking at the stars and at a spacecraft whose solar panels were very bright.

"To get back to what we were discussing before," the publisher resumed, pacing up and down, "the only thing that matters is the result, don't you think?"

Jack ground out his butt with his sandal and nodded agreement. I did too, but no one asked my opinion. The three of us were facing the river, which became wider all at once between the Lauzon headland and the Anse de Beauport, dividing in two to embrace the Île d'Orléans. The landscape was immense, almost too vast, and it was hard to gaze at it without thinking about the big sailing ships that had left Saint-Malo or La Rochelle in the 16th century to look for Eldorado or a lost paradise. For me, all that beauty spreading out as far as the eye could see gave me the feeling that where the heart is concerned, my country was Quebec.

"It's quite wonderful on this terrace," said the publisher. "Do you ever come out here to write?"

"Writing outside is for the young," said Jack. "I only come out to read or to dream or to watch over Gabrielle when she's in her room. But I could never write here, there would be too many distractions: the boats, the clouds, the swallows..."

"Yet you've written all over the place, at roadsides and in campgrounds when you went to California in the Volkswagen minibus."

"I was in better shape back then."

"The book still sells very well," said the publisher. "People are still buying it."

"That's their problem!" said Jack.

His face had taken on a woeful look, which was a bad sign. The publisher tried to give him a little self-confidence.

"A man in search of his brother was a good subject," he said in a voice that was nearly lilting, so badly did he want to encourage Jack.

"Oh yes, his brother Majorque..."

I was shocked. The brother Majorque wasn't in his book, he was in a novel by Gabrielle entitled *De quoi t'ennuies-tu, Éveline?* I didn't even dare to look at the publisher's face, which must have been totally distraught. What's next, he must have been wondering, as was I, if old Jack had started to confuse his characters with those created by another writer?

10

Tender Is the Night

The store had been closed for a while, night was falling, and I was in bed with Charabia and a science fiction book, *The Game-Players of Titan*, by Philip K. Dick.

I wasn't crazy about that kind of writing, which was very popular with readers of my age, but this book was the right one that evening, for two reasons: I wanted to change worlds, as my own was a little monotonous; and I'd been hooked by the first sentence: *It had been a terrible night, and when he tried to drive home he had a terrible argument with his car.*

"Mr. Garden, you are in no condition to drive. Please use the auto-auto mech and recline in the rear seat."

When I was starting the third chapter, young Charabia abruptly jumped off my stomach and ran to the store. I thought that the cat, unable to sleep because of the way my stomach shook when the book made me laugh, was going to take refuge in a spot that was usually peaceful — the top drawer of Jack's desk, which we left partly open for that purpose.

I had resumed my reading when I thought I heard sounds coming from the store. Intrigued and vaguely worried, I put down my book and got up to investigate. Just as I was about to leave the Parenthesis, stark naked, I noticed some mysterious lights and shadows running around the wall. I pulled on my jeans and my grey sweater, telling myself that since there was no fire in the stove, the glow might come from the flashlight of a burglar who wanted to grab the cash. Or that it was Jack who was having problems with his neurons.

I was wrong. What I caught sight of when I walked into the store thrilled me and will be etched forever on my heart. Mist was back — my little sister, one-half of my soul — and she had in her hands a kind of illuminated carousel that turned on a pivot. With infinite care she set it down on the counter. I was so filled with wonder that I couldn't say a word. Approaching it, I saw that the carousel, which was made of copper or maybe brass, had six horses; they moved around with the pretty tinkling of little bells set off by the heat that rose from some candles set into the base.

Charabia leaped onto the counter without a sound. He seemed to be on the verge of holding out a paw towards a candle-flame but he stopped and lay down, his front paws folded in the manner of monks who bury their hands in the sleeves of their habits. He looked sometimes at the carousel, sometimes at the enlarged shadow of the horses that ran along the walls and on the books around us.

Mist had on a long white linen dress with birds embroidered at the neck and on the sleeves. From her rather melancholy smile, I realized that the carousel was supposed to erase the feeling of abandonment that I'd had while she was away. Leaning with my elbows on the counter across from her, I discovered something that in my agitation I hadn't noticed: she had glitter and coloured stars stuck to her face. When I kissed her one of the tiny stars adhered to my lower lip; to take it off, she wet the tip of her index finger and moved it very delicately along my lip.

"Thank you," I said.

Like a child I could have spent hours looking at the candle flames, the circling of the golden horses, the giant shadows, and the shining eyes of Mistassini. I don't know how long we stayed there face to face, still and silent... All at once my sister collapsed.

I sped around the counter. She was lying on her back, unconscious, one leg folded under her; she had on moccasins.

"Mist?"

Panicking, I repeated her name several times. I unfolded her leg but didn't know exactly what to do. I'd seen people in movies slapping the hand or cheek of a person who'd fainted and in westerns, even flinging a bucket of water in their face. I patted her hand gently, to no effect, and I didn't dare to slap her cheek for fear of hurting her. I thought of asking for help, but I couldn't decide if it would be better to call an ambulance or the police or old Jack.

Trying to think, I switched on the lamp on Jack's desk and blew out the candles on the carousel. The shadows galloping across the walls disappeared and there was a temporary lull in my head. I decided I could manage on my own. Though she was very pale, Mist didn't seem to be suffering from an injury or a serious malaise: she was breathing normally and she wasn't having convulsions. Standing behind her, I gripped her under her armpits in an attempt to get her on her feet. It was impossible, her body was too limp, so I simply dragged her into the Parenthesis, where I managed to settle her on my mattress which I'd placed on the floor. Her moccasins had fallen off along the way.

As her face was nearly as white as her dress, I placed a pillow under her legs to stimulate her circulation. Then I thought of something very simple: I opened the fridge, took out an ice-cube, and pressed it to her forehead and temples. She came to and looked at me, seeming lost.

"We're in the bookstore in Vieux-Québec," I said. "There's nothing to worry about."

She let me know that she understood but there was still some fog in her blue eyes.

"You came here with a beautiful carousel that was all lit up, and horses that went around in a circle, and shadows that galloped along the walls of books. It was gorgeous. Charabia and I were admiring it when all at once you passed out."

"Ah yes!" she breathed.

She remembered. I left her for a moment to pour a saucer of milk for the cat who'd come running when he heard the fridge door open. She tried to get up but as her face was still very pale, I advised her not to move.

"So you carried me in here?" she asked.

"Of course," I said.

"I wasn't too heavy?"

"Not in the least!"

The lie could probably be seen on my face so I turned my back on my sister and went to fetch her moccasins, which were lying next to Jack's desk. Coming back, I noticed that she was palpating her stomach with her fingertips. I bent over her.

"Did you eat anything today?"

"No," she said, "I totally forgot."

"I'll fix something."

"That's nice, but it's late."

"Not all that late. I'm overjoyed you're here, I love the carousel you brought me and I'm really glad that you aren't sick."

To conclude my declaration, an unusually long one for me, I bent down a little more and rubbed my nose against hers, which in our code meant: "For the rest of our lives and even beyond the grave." My goal was to make her smile and it worked. Next I suggested a bowl of soup. I'm an expert at mixing packaged soups. I've tried several recipes over the years and I can assure you that you get excellent results if you combine chicken noodle and pureed vegetable soups.

First I put a litre of water on to boil.

"Can you take the pillow out from under my legs?" asked Mist.

"Of course," I said.

"I feel a little better..."

"Anyway you aren't as pale as you were a while ago."

"My stomach's gurgling, actually I think I'm very hungry."

"I'm sure that's why you fainted."

I took away the pillow and helped her sit up on the mattress with her back against the wall, then I returned to my hot-plate. Gradually, I poured the package of dehydrated chicken noodle soup into the simmering water, waited patiently for five minutes, stirring now and then with my wooden spoon, then added the vegetable soup a little at a time to avoid lumps.

"That smells good!" said Mist. "It smells like home..."

She fell silent and closed her eyes. We rarely alluded to the past — it was a tacit agreement between us — but I was sure that she, like me, was thinking about the Sunday morning when she was still a teenager and had left the house on a sudden impulse. At the time we were living in a village on the edge of a river; on the other side there was a forest so vast that we didn't know where it ended. The village was a world of its own, it contained everything we needed for growing up: dogs and cats, friends, playgrounds, and strange adults who were good at telling stories.

We had everything we needed, yet on that summer morning my little sister had gone away. She had eaten with the rest of us and then, taking from her closet a knapsack she'd already packed, and saying that she had a world to see, she'd set off down the hill that ran along the tennis court, her blonde head barely showing above the huge khaki pack. I followed her with my eyes, posted at a window in the shed that was covered with spider webs. When she got to the main street she simply held out her thumb and a minute later, got into a red pickup truck.

Her departure had taken us by surprise. My little sister was a normal girl: she climbed trees, she skated on the frozen river, in tennis she had a two-handed backhand that allowed her to get hold of the ball very quickly, like Martina Hingis. On the other hand, it's true that she spent hours reading and that at times she seemed absent or lost, walled inside herself, but no one suspected that she had so fierce a will.

I let the soup rest for a moment, then I dipped two ladlefuls into a big bowl; it was steaming and the bowl burned my fingers.

"Just a second!" I said.

Taking two ice cubes from the freezer compartment, I put them in the bowl. The soup overflowed as a result, but I'd been sensible enough to stand the bowl in the sink. I tasted a few spoonfuls to be sure that it wasn't too hot, then I took the bowl to Mist. Her hands were shaking so I knelt beside her on the mattress and started to feed her, bringing the spoon to her mouth. She smiled between spoonfuls and even though she didn't say anything, I was sure that she remembered when she was little.

When there was just a drop of soup left, she took the bowl from me and set it on the floor for Charabia, who was circling around us. A few seconds later, she closed her eyes, her head dipped to one side and very slowly, while she was clutching the pillow with both hands, the top of her body toppled onto the mattress. I picked up the empty bowl and switched off the lamp.

She was asleep. By the little glow from a nearby apartment that came in through the skylight, I saw that her sleep was very agitated, so I lay down behind her and put my arm around her waist. Instinctively, she pressed herself against my stomach, then her breathing slowed down and became more regular. I'm a little taller than she is and my cheek was resting against her short hair that smelled of camomile.

I refrained from moving so I wouldn't waken her. It was impossible for me to sleep, but I was happy to have my little sister back, to hold her in my arms, to feel the curves of her body merge with mine and to whisper in her ear, knowing that she couldn't hear them, words that I could not say aloud.

In the middle of the night, my shoulder was stiff so I freed my arm from around her waist, got up without a sound and went to pace in the bookstore, which was lit by the streetlamps outside. I listened for a moment to the murmur of the books, then I couldn't resist an urge to light the candles on the carousel. At once the golden horses began again to turn around with the tinkling sound of little bells, casting black shadows onto the walls, and bringing back to my mind a very old song that Jack had taught me, which tells of the king's horses that come running to drink together at a river that ran down the middle of the bed.

On the counter next to the cash register sat a book that I took into the Parenthesis. It was J. D. Salinger's *Catcher in the Rye*.

I got back in bed next to Mist, putting my arm around her again, my knees in the hollow of hers, and my nose in her short hair; she made a sound like a contented murmur. I was overcome by sleep. Several ideas were going through my head, in disorder and in shreds... The fridge held everything we needed for breakfast, including several sorts of jam — strawberry, blueberry, and apricot — and there was peanut butter in the cupboard, which was lucky... My sister and I were both searching for something, for a kind of paradise that could exist beyond intimacy, but we didn't know exactly what it was or how to attain it... First there was *Treasure Island*, now Jack had left a second book for me. I didn't know why he was doing it but he must have had something in mind...

It was still night and I'd been sleeping for a while, dreaming that it was winter and that we were crossing the white and frozen river in our old village on our way into the forest when Mist sat up suddenly, at the same time waking me. Sitting up on the little mattress, she took my hand and ran it over her forehead which was soaked in sweat. She turned onto her side, asked me to undo the zipper on her dress, then pulled it over her head in a movement made languid by sleep that I thought was very beautiful. The angles and curves of her body were familiar to me, but it was a pleasure and a gift from the gods to see them again, especially in the half-light that gave them a mysterious appearance.

Mist turned to face me. I pulled the sheet over us, holding my breath. With her face close to mine she started to trace with her finger my eyebrows, then the bridge of my nose, and around my mouth, as if she were drawing me, and she completed her action by pressing the palm of her hand over my eyes; the curved party of her hand fit my eye socket precisely.

She kissed me on the cheek, next to the ear, and her lips slipped to the hollow of my shoulder. I paid attention to everything that was happening, in particular to the quivering that started on my neck and rippled down to the small of my back. For a moment, she rested her head on my shoulder and I thought that she was resting. Opening my eyes, I was a little disappointed to see that hers were already closed and that her breathing was slower and deeper. I had got used to the idea that she was going to go on with her caresses: that is what we need most — caresses — yet they're the hardest thing to ask for.

Snuggling against me, utterly exhausted, she slept. Gradually I turned onto my back. I kept watch. I dozed now and then. Through the skylight I could see stars whose names I didn't know. Mist was moving in her sleep: she threw one knee across my legs, put one hand on my hip, moved her head back onto my chest. A little later Charabia joined us and lay on my stomach.

It was more or less in this position that Jack found us the next morning around half-past nine. Someone had told him that the bookstore wasn't open yet and he had worried about me. Actually I'd only stayed in bed so that Mist could sleep as long as possible, I swear. Seeing us in one another's arms he looked relieved; he got down on his knees and being careful not to wake her, he kissed my little sister on the temple, in the place where her blonde hair was shortest. Every time he approached her, touched her, my heart sank a little. He murmured that she was as beautiful as an angel: that was all he said, then he went to look after the bookstore.

He served customers as long as Mist was still asleep. He didn't reproach me either before he left or when he came back in the evening to have supper with us. He knew practically nothing about cooking but in Mist's honour he had baked a butterscotch pie that was still warm.

When I walked him back home after supper, he began to set out an idea in such a roundabout way and so indecisively that I couldn't tell what he was getting at. We arrived at rue Couillard, which went straight to his apartment, but he decided to detour via the Côte de la Fabrique, my favourite street.

"Know what you ought to do?" he asked.

"No," I said.

"You ought to take a trip."

My first reaction was to think that he may have wanted to get me away from Mist. But really, that wasn't like him.

"Why?" I asked.

"To knock some sense into you!" he said, laughing. Then he turned serious again.

"No," he said. "It's to have a good supply of images."

"What for?"

"For when you want to do something inventive (that's the word he used most often instead of *creative*, which he thought was pretentious). The images we invent, for instance when we write, are the reflections of those that lie dormant deep inside us. Do you understand?"

"Not really," I said.

"That's alright. I don't understand myself."

At the top of La Fabrique he led me across rue Buade, then I went with him into Giguère's cigar store. He checked out the contents of a few magazines, but nothing seemed to interest him so he bought a bar of dark chocolate and left. Then we headed towards rue des Remparts. I wanted to know more about what he had in mind.

"So you think I ought to travel?"

"That's right," he said.

"Where to?"

"France for instance?"

"I went there when I was a student. I spent a few days in Paris, then I went to see the Grand Prix de Monaco and I visited the Côte d'Azur by moped; I even got as far as Les Saintes-Maries-de-la-Mer."

Apparently Jack had some things to explain to me, because he lit a cigarette and suggested another detour, via Parc Montmorency. I was then bombarded with questions that he didn't give me time to answer. In the south of France had I taken the time to visit the small villages in Provence? On the Côte d'Azur had I stopped at Lavendou and Cassis? Had I seen the pilgrimage of the Gypsies? In Paris, had I seen the Medicis fountain, the Passage Choiseul, the Lapin Agile, the Cité Florale, the Butte-aux-Cailles?

With an ease that surprised me, he listed a good many other places I'd never heard of, then he asked how long my trip had been. All in all, I'd only stayed for three weeks. In his opinion that wasn't long enough: you only know a country if you share the people's everyday lives for some months. Obviously that was more expensive, but he had friends in the 12th arrondissement who could put me up for free. And if I wanted to visit other parts of France cheaply, he knew a newspaper in which individuals advertised used mini-buses at a moderate price. As for other expenses, part would be covered by my translation work and he would take care of the rest.

We arrived across from his place on rue des Remparts, and I was still wondering, apprehensively, if he was serious and why he was offering me this trip. Did he really want to take me away from my little sister? Did he want me to incur a debt towards him and feel obliged to give him the "little push" he'd alluded to one night in the Italian restaurant on rue Sainte-Angèle?

All that was running through my head. I had things to think about. I gave him a sidelong glance, trying to get the beginning of an answer, but his thoughts were floating above my earthly concerns: once again he was looking up at Gabrielle's window.

11

A Cat on the Head

Jack's friends in Paris had a three-room apartment on a pedestrian street in the 12th arrondissement, rue Villa Saint-Mandé.

He had told me that the place was quiet. That was true: the sound of cars on the nearby boulevards was reduced to a distant hum, but he'd forgotten to say that the apartment was too small for three people. I slept on the living-room sofa. I had to wait to go to bed until they'd finished watching TV; they were fond of the late-night shows, especially the ones featuring a table of authors talking about their books. But they hadn't even asked if Jack was still writing or if his books were doing well. Maybe they, like many people, thought that what they saw on TV was more important than real life.

In the morning, to disturb them as little as possible, I got up when they did. Though both were retired, they got up on the stroke of seven. An elderly, slightly deaf woman upstairs listened to the first news broadcast on her clock radio, so the day got off to a noisy start. After a breakfast of *biscottes* and *café au lait,* I took a few things and went to the neighbourhood library. Settled on the third floor where there were long tables and all kinds of dictionaries and encyclopedias, I began my day by doing some translation, which allowed me afterwards to stroll around until evening with my mind at rest.

First, I explored the neighbourhood. What surprised me most, aside from the large number of old people, many of them walking along behind a dog that was pulling on its leash, was that just a few steps from my building there was every imaginable service: bus, Métro, post office, bookstore, barbershop, pharmacy, bakery, shoe repair, bistro, newspapers, bank, food, doctors, hospital... After a few days I would be aware that behind this profusion of activities another life was hidden, a tranquil and original life that could be found in courtyards, gardens, and at the ends of passages and alleyways.

But I wasn't there yet. For the time being I was content to discover, like everyone else, the squares, the monuments, the commemorative plaques, as well as the habits and ways of behaving that made up people's everyday lives. This didn't stop me from having a few little adventures. One day around noon, for instance, as I was walking past a bistro at the top of the rue du Rendez-Vous, I took a very violent blow on my head; my knees bent and I saw stars like in the comics. At first I thought that a flowerpot had fallen from a balcony and landed on my skull. I looked around: no broken pieces on the sidewalk. All I saw was a ginger cat. The bistro door was open: the cat slithered inside, practically crawling, and huddled under a table in the corner.

I followed it in.

On the right was a half-moon shaped counter, with a barman drying dishes behind it. Apparently he hadn't seen what had happened.

"Monsieur?" he asked.

"I've just been hit on the head by a cat," I declared.

Immediately, I realized that still in shock, I'd muttered something incomprehensible. And since I'd pointed to the top of my head, I must have looked like one of the Tintin characters Dupont and Dupond.

"*Pardon*?" asked the barman politely.

A couple of lovers were sitting at a table. Leaning on the counter an elderly man was reading *L'Équipe*.

"I was walking past the bistro and a cat fell on my head," I explained, being careful to pronounce every syllable.

"It did? On your head?" the barman repeated. He turned around to look at the big clock above the bar. He obviously thought that I'd had too much to drink and that such a spectacle so early in the day was a pitiful sight. But the elderly man intervened.

"I saw a cat come in," he confirmed. "Look, there he is, under the table!"

The barman leaned across the counter and the two lovers turned their heads to see what the reader of *L'Équipe* had pointed at. The ginger cat was still huddled under the table at the back, his fur bristling, eyes bulging: he was quite young and he was paralyzed with fear.

"But .... that's the barber's cat!" exclaimed the barman.

"You're right," said the elderly man. "Oh là là! He fell from the third floor! We must tell Monsieur Antoine!"

"I'll call him," said the barman. He dialled a number on the bar phone and while the person who'd answered was telling the person concerned, the clients were saying more and more, featuring a good many *Oh là là!*s. I understood that Monsieur Antoine, who lived on the third floor, had a barbershop on an adjacent street and that his cat had the dangerous habit of sleeping among the potted flowers and shrubs that adorned the wrought-iron balcony.

The barber burst inside and took me fervently in his arms. Tall and hefty, he had what is commonly called a "leonine head." I was impressed. His black smock, on which some blonde hairs were still caught, showed that he'd left his work in great haste.

"That reminds me, I hope you weren't injured. How do you feel?" he asked, moving back a step.

"I'm fine, thank you," I said.

"Do you want us to take you to the hospital?"

"No, that's not necessary."

A half-dozen people had come into the bistro and everyone, suddenly concerned, gave me a questioning look. Then my shyness led me to exaggerate, as usual. I declared that I'd never felt so well in all my life; that the blow to my skull had probably wakened the half of my brain that had been working in slow motion; that we Québécois were used to standing up to the cold, the Anglos, the Iroquois, and the wild animals in our vast forests, we had solid heads and it would take more than a cat on the cranium to floor us.

"Ah! You're *Canadien!*" exclaimed Monsieur Antoine.

"Yes," I said.

Canadien was not the word I'd have chosen, but having myself launched into a tirade devoid of any subtlety, I couldn't expect more subtlety from him.

"Now where's my cat?" he asked abruptly.

"Under the table at the back," said the barman.

Monsieur Antoine went over to the table, placed one knee on the floor, and spoke to the cat in a little singsong voice that contrasted with his imposing physique. The cat, still in a daze or disconcerted by his new environment, refused to budge but he did allow his master to stretch out his hand to feel him and pet him.

"He isn't hurt. He's scared, that's all."

"I'm so glad!" I said.

"You saved his life. That deserves a drink!"

Reassured as to the health of his cat, he led me to the bar and offered me a drink. At the third *pastis* he became very talkative and told me that he came from around Caen, in Normandy, and that his grandparents had cheered the *Canadiens* who'd taken part in the Allied landing. He pulled me by the arm to show me a map of France on the wall near the toilets. Warmed up by the *pastis*, I asserted that it's a small world, because my own grandfather had been with the Canadian troops who had landed on the Normandy coast, that his group was called the Chaudière Regiment, and that my grandfather had been a lieutenant-colonel.

He was flabbergasted.

I declared in one breath that my grandfather and the men in his regiment had landed on the beach at Bernières-sur-Mer on June 6, 1944, and that they'd gone on to capture the villages of Bény-sur-Mer, Basly, and Colomby-sur-Thaon.

The people in the bistro were stunned.

I was well on my way to becoming the biggest liar in the 12th arrondissement.

12

An Adieu in the Métro

I had just arrived on the platform of the Picpus station when the Métro, heralded by a muffled rumble and by a yellow glow on the walls, emerged from the tunnel and clanked to a stop. The car that had stopped in front of me was full of people so I made my way towards the next one. It was crammed too and I had to stand. To get some rest and to absorb the jolts from the rattling car, I leaned my back against one of the metal posts that you could hold onto during the ride.

That day a fine, persistent rain was falling over Paris. There had been a number of grey or rainy days since my arrival. I couldn't hold it against the old city, since the grey of the sky was offset by the already green foliage of the chestnut trees and plane trees and by the bright colours of the awnings, the boutique windows, and the flowerbeds.

The rain had given me an urge to go for a ride in the Métro. I had decided to take line six to the Arc de Triomphe, then line two back to my neighbourhood: if you placed the two lines with their aerial sections end to end, you would circle the city.

From where I was, I could see a man and woman embracing. At first, feeling awkward, I observed their intermittent reflection in a window of the Métro, then having ascertained that they were in a world where nothing could disturb them, I started to watch them directly.

They were around thirty. Indifferent to the people around them, they held hands, exchanged loving looks, kissed and cuddled. Now and then the man broke off what he was doing to say something to his ladyfriend. I didn't hear every word but I was surprised to see the light that shone on the woman's face, as sweet and warm as honey.

The Métro crossed the Seine and when we arrived at the Quai-de-la-Gare station, the lovebirds held each other very tightly. The man murmured something more into the woman's ear, then he lifted a leather briefcase that I hadn't noticed, stood up, and left the car.

The woman didn't take her eyes off him for a moment and I turned my head to watch him. He took a few steps on the platform, through the group of people, then he turned around. He was tall with dark, curly hair and he was beaming. Holding his briefcase he waved *adieu* to his friend who sat in the same place and continued to look at him through the window. She smiled and you could still see the warm light pouring onto her face.

The train started up. After one last glance at the deserted platform the woman began to look vaguely into space. I was relieved to see that in spite of everything, she didn't look unhappy. She still wore a half-smile and I realized that at this moment, she was not alone:

her friend's affection was keeping her company. But the light on her face was beginning to fade.

That light was the trace of the man, it was all that remained of him. And so, though I didn't know why, that trace, in itself insignificant, became very precious to me.

At the next station, the luminous trace dwindled again. A little farther along, at the Glacière station, the woman got up, and just as she was leaving to blend into the crowd, I saw that her face now was inscrutable and as devoid of light as those of the other passengers.

Banal though it was, the incident made a strong impression on me. It was still on my mind when the train, after a long route underground, crossed the Seine again by the Bir-Hakeim bridge. In the middle of it, I could make out through the curtain of rain a replica of the Statue of Liberty, which reminded me of a suspense film in which Harrison Ford was trying desperately to find his wife, who'd been kidnapped by Russian spies. Farther along, the Métro plunged once again into the entrails of the city. When it came back up I could see some places that I'd explored in the past, which bore well-known names like Pigalle, La Chapelle, Belleville, Ménilmontant. In some neighbourhoods though, throngs of people in brightly coloured djellabas were making their way through market stalls that overflowed onto the sidewalks, and none of it resembled the images I'd held in my memory.

When the Métro left me off at the Nation station in my neighbourhood, the rain had lessened but not the deep sorrow that I'd felt when I saw the light fading from the face of the unknown woman. I shopped for food at the Marché Casino, then went home. I wasn't living with Jack's friends anymore. It had become gradually clear to me that even by observing a very strict schedule for my comings and goings — phoning if I was going to be at all late, contributing to household expenses, not leaving my belongings

lying around, in a word, by making myself as small as I could —
I was still a big nuisance. They had their own habits, their own
quirks, and no room had been set aside for me in their well-ordered
existence. I'd finally left and since then I had been living in the
Volkswagen minibus.

The incongruous notion of moving into a vehicle in Paris to
pursue my exploration of the city had been imposed on me by
the situation. When I announced to my hosts at breakfast one
morning that it was time for me to go, they thought about Jack.
They recalled that way back when, he had left them and set off on
a long trip around France and Europe, and that they'd helped
him out by tracking down a used camper in the classified ads in a
magazine. What was the name of it, that magazine that came out
every week? While they were searching their memories I heard
myself say that such a journey was exactly what I had in mind.
Instead of following the advice of Epictetus who said: "Should
you find yourself alone among strangers, remain silent," I had
maintained that I was already delighted at the prospect of travelling
in the regions of France, so beautiful and varied, at the wheel of a
minibus, that at the same time would serve as accommodation, and
that I'd have time to sell it again before I went back to Quebec.

Between two *biscottes*, Jack's friends had suddenly remembered
that the magazine was called *La Centrale des particuliers*. And then
without finishing their bowls of *café au lait*, acting as if there were
an emergency, they went out and walked me to the newsstand on
the little square at the top of boulevard de Picpus. Introducing me
to the saleswoman, they explained where I came from and what
I wanted and they paid for the magazine themselves. I was lucky:
La Centrale came out on Thursday and it was that very day!

Someone living in Créteil, a nearby suburb, was offering for 1500
euros a raised minibus outfitted for camping, whose body "needed

work." When I got there, my first impression of the Volks was bad: it had definitely been hit in the rear because the metal was dented and rusty, and the motor panel didn't close.

Contrary to all logic, I decided to buy it anyway, after a brief road test. Jack's friends advanced me the money.

The interior layout, though basic, I liked a lot. Thanks to the raised roof, I could stand in the space between the kitchen nook and the seat. According to Jack, the standing position was the one most appropriate for a translator who is constantly moving to consult the dictionaries and reference books spread out around him.

And so it was to the Volkswagen minibus that I made my way that night, after I'd spent part of the day looking out from the aerial Métro at the rain-filled sky that was pouring every shade of grey onto walls, clothes, and faces. The Volks was parked on boulevard de Picpus, not far from Courteline Square and practically across from the Hôtel du Printemps.

The choice of that spot was not the fruit of lengthy research. I'd been driving around the neighbourhood haphazardly, avoiding one-way streets and wary about giving right of way to vehicles coming from the right, when I saw a parking space that had just become free and I stopped for a moment to think. In the end, I stayed there, lacking the courage to look elsewhere. The Volks was sheltered beneath the trees and half-concealed by delivery vans; on the left there was a garden full of flowers and a playground for children; and I was quite fond of the Hôtel du Printemps because, glancing indiscreetly into the lobby, I'd spotted a fake electric fireplace with glowing red logs that resembled the one in my parents' living room when I was a little boy.

When I got to my new abode, which was painted green and beige, I was relieved to see that there wasn't a ticket on the windshield. I got inside and didn't slam the door. My bag of groceries contained a can of pumpkin soup, a package of Mousline instant mashed potatoes, a tin of tuna in olive oil, and some tomatoes; but my bad luck, I'd forgotten dessert.

I drank a little muscat wine to warm my bones that were chilled from the humid air, then I lit the gas and put the soup on to heat. The bluish flame made me think about the luminous trail I'd seen gradually extinguished from the face of the young woman on the Métro, and suddenly I realized that during this entire rainy day, though I hadn't admitted it to myself, I had been missing my little sister Mistassini and the light that shone in her blue eyes.

13

In Search of Shakespeare and Company

The weather had been fine for a few days and I was glad to be free of the customs and the unwritten laws of Jack's friends.

Every morning, to celebrate my newfound independence I went to the bakery at the corner of rue Marsoulan and bought two croissants and made myself some real orange juice. Before settling down with my translations, I often took some time to write to Mist and tell her what had happened to me the day before.

The post office was right next door on boulevard de Picpus and one day when I went there to mail a letter, I was lucky enough to meet the letter carrier who was setting out on her rounds in the neighbourhood. Her name was Françoise. I'd met her at Jack's friends' place, where she delivered the mail to letterboxes at the foot of the staircase; we'd got along well, because she dreamed of visiting the "great open spaces" of Quebec. I walked a few steps along the boulevard with her, and when I showed her where I was living now, she promised she'd bring my mail as often as possible.

I felt light-hearted then when I boarded the 86 bus to get to 74, rue du Cardinal-Lemoine, in the 5th arrondissement. I had read in *A Moveable Feast* that Hemingway had lived at that address. It was a kind of pilgrimage that I wanted to make on Jack's behalf, but on my own as well; old Jack loved Hemingway because of his writing, which he considered to be "strong and concise, like a closed fist," while I, who knew nothing or practically nothing in the field and who had a tendency to lie, I loved him instead for the honesty he put into his work.

After crossing the Seine on the Sully bridge, of which one pillar stood on the tip of the Île Saint-Louis, the bus let me off at the corner of rue des Écoles. I started going up to rue du Cardinal-Lemoine rather slowly, because even though the slope was not very steep I felt a kind of fatigue in my legs and a lump in my throat. At number 74, a plaque above a door freshly painted in blue, gave the following information.

> *From January 22, 1922 to August 23, 1923 the American writer Ernest* HEMINGWAY, *1899-1961, lived on the third floor of this building with his wife Hadley. This neighbourhood was the true birthplace of his work and of his characteristically spare style.*

A group of tourists made me decamp. Shortly after I came to the Place de la Contrescarpe. I sat down at the first terrace and ordered a *café-crème*, being careful to enunciate clearly the last syllable so that the waiter wouldn't ask me to repeat the word. The Contrescarpe was a very pretty square of modest proportions, made cheerful by bright red awnings, and I knew that Hemingway had described it in *A Moveable Feast*. I had the book in my knap-sack, along with a package of cookies filled with orange cream and a half-bottle of mineral water, but a voice was telling me that it would be best not to draw any comparison between what was written and what was real. All at once an image of Jack was super-imposed on that of Hemingway. I remembered the "little push" but I chased it out of my mind.

I paid for my coffee, then went back to look at the building where Hemingway had lived when he was young. There were four windows on the third floor, all closed, all the same, and even if I positioned myself on the sidewalk across the street to study them, I couldn't tell which one was that of the writer's apartment.

How could I find out? If Mist had been there she wouldn't have hesitated for a second, so I decided to go inside and ring the concierge's bell. I went up to the blue door and ... there was a keypad with a digital code! Very disappointed, not knowing what to do next, I was already walking away when a rather corpulent woman with bleached blonde hair appeared, carrying a purse and dragging a small cloth-covered shopping cart with a baguette stick-ing out.

She hadn't seen me.

"*Pardon, Madame,* may I go inside with you?" I asked behind her back. Startled, the woman turned around. She hugged her purse against her heart.

"Why, may I ask? Don't you know the code?"

"I don't live here."

"Are you coming to see someone?"

She looked me up and down. I examined her in turn but more discreetly. Her hair wasn't blonde, it was white with a faint pink tinge. She seemed refined, had impeccable diction, and a gentle, tired smile.

"No, I've come for the apartment," I said.

"As far as I know there's no apartment for rent..."

"I meant Hemingway's apartment. I'd like to know exactly where he lived."

"On the third floor."

"Yes, but which window?"

The woman had raised her arm to punch in the code. She stopped midway, looked at me with what seemed to be compassion, and I felt as if I were at most fifteen years old.

"Ssshh!" she said. "It's a secret!"

"Why is that?"

"All the third-floor tenants are writers. Very young writers, still unknown. But they're all convinced that they live in your Hemingway's apartment. It stimulates them, so we mustn't disabuse them. Don't you agree, young man?"

Without waiting for an answer, she entered a number that I didn't have time to note and then very quickly, lifting her cart, she pushed open the door which closed right away. Dumbfounded, arms dangling, I stood all alone on the sidewalk with the woman's words echoing in my head. After a moment, I admitted that she was right and started back down the street.

While I was walking, I took Hemingway's book out of my knapsack. I wanted to find the route he took when his work was done and he let himself wander at random along the sloping streets towards the Quartier Latin and the quays of the Seine. It was fairly simple: he would take a cross street that led him to the "windswept" Place du Panthéon and a little farther along, he would cross the Jardin du Luxembourg where at the time the museum exhibited Impres-sionist paintings; then he would go to Shakespeare and Company, the bookstore at 12, rue de l'Odéon, where in the late afternoon, he might run into James Joyce.

I had no trouble finding rue de l'Odéon. At number 12, though, there was no bookstore: there was a boutique selling clothes imported from China. I looked in the book to see if I'd mistaken the number ... no, this was it.

A glance at the window of the boutique, then I went inside.

The single room, square and small, was filled with long racks from which hung Chinese dresses, tunics, and pants. In a corner behind a table placed diagonally sat a Chinese woman who was certainly old enough to be a grandmother.

She sent an encouraging smile my way. I stepped up, slightly intimidated by the fact that the racks held nothing but women's garments. When I said *bonjour* she answered something that sounded like *ni-bao*. She was really very old, with wrinkles that formed stars at the corners of her eyes and around her mouth. It would not be easy to explain why I was there.

To show her that I was looking for a bookstore, I drew some imaginary shelves on the nearest wall, then I mimed taking books from a shelf. The woman's smile grew broader and new stars appeared on her face, but it was clear that she didn't understand what I was doing. So then I showed her Hemingway's book, keeping my index finger on the author's name. She screwed up her eyes and looked at the cover that showed a man with a cigarette in his lips, hair slicked back, dressed for a *bal musette*. Then, with her eyes nearly closed, she studied the name that I'd pointed to. Her face remained impassive: either she didn't know Hemingway or she could only read Chinese.

Short of ideas, I left the grandmother and went back out on the street. She had shown me to the door, saying something that sounded like *tsaï-djien*, and as I was taking one last look at the building I suddenly spied on the first floor a plaque so small that I hadn't seen it when I arrived. It read:

Jacques Poulin

IN 1922,

IN THIS HOUSE,

SYLVIA BEACH PUBLISHED

"ULYSSES"

BY JAMES JOYCE

I hadn't been wrong about the address, but that was slim consolation. What had become of Shakespeare and Company, with its big stove that warmed writers and readers during the winter months? Where had Sylvia Beach, who owned the bookstore, gone, with her "lively sharply sculptured face, brown eyes that were as alive as a small animal's and as gay as a young girl's"? While I was heading for the Seine to stroll the quays for a while, I was thinking about the warmth that suffused the books old or new there, mending broken hearts, giving hope to novice writers, and I thought to myself that all that warmth, human or artificial, couldn't have disappeared without a trace.

After crossing the Place Saint-Michel, where there were too many tourists and cops, I started along the quays towards the east, stopping here and there to examine the books and posters in the *bouquinistes'* dark green stalls, or to admire beyond the swollen yellow water of the Seine, the imposing silhouette of Notre-Dame, firmly supported on her flying buttresses.

Just as I stepped on a stone staircase on the other side of rue du Petit-Pont to go down to the banks of the Seine I felt a pang when I spotted on my right, set back and lower down, a big sign on which stood out in black letters on a pale yellow background, the words I'd lost all hope of seeing again: Shakespeare and Company.

The bookstore had moved to 37, rue de la Bûcherie. The front and the inside were lit up and, as Jack had told me, the light seemed to come from the books themselves. Drawing closer, I saw that volumes were overflowing outside the store, in boxes and on shelves. I spied through the window a room with low tables, books all the way up to the ceiling, dark varnished beams, a chandelier with several branches: all was calm and restful to the eyes. Inside, my pleasure grew even more: there was a series of narrow corridors with piles of books in every corner, even around an old washbasin, and I breathed in the aroma of old paper.

It was a haven of silence, warmth, and memory. Night was falling when I left the place, at the invitation of a man with white hair and a face like parchment, whose presence I hadn't noticed because his suit was the same faded colour as books that have stayed on shelves too long. He wanted to know if I'd found what I was looking for and I replied in the affirmative. I had found in the centre of Paris, across from Notre-Dame, a remnant of the human warmth that had soothed the hearts of some young writers who'd come from America, like Hemingway, F. Scott Fitzgerald, and the other members of the lost generation.

14

The Bois de Vincennes

Sitting in my Volks on boulevard de Picpus, I just had to raise my head and I could see, perched some thirty metres high on one of the two stone columns framing avenue du Trône near the Place de la Nation, King Philippe Auguste, who was looking in my direction. It was reassuring to know that I was under the protection of a king of France, yet I was thinking of leaving this spot.

Not that I disliked the neighbourhood. For instance, I was always happy to receive the mail that Françoise slipped into the top of the passenger side window, which I left open a few centimetres so it could serve as a mail slot. One morning I'd received a padded envelope from Jack: his handwriting, very erratic, was easy to recognize. In the envelope was a collection of short stories by Raymond Carver, *Where I'm Calling From*. There was nothing else, not even an explanatory note. This was the third time, it seemed to me, that Jack had intervened in my reading, and I was fairly sure that he had a precise idea in mind for each book. With Carver, whose work I loved, it was obviously the extreme sobriety of the writing; with Salinger, undoubtedly the tone; and with Stevenson, the life.

Every day before I started to translate, wearing earplugs to keep out distractions, I kept an eye out for someone else I was glad to see: a municipal employee in fluorescent green coveralls whose job was to push garbage into the gutter with a twig broom; when his broom slapped the water it produced a rhythmical sound that reminded me of the sound of waves at the seaside.

I was getting to know the inhabitants of the neighbourhood. If I saw a dog pulling on his leather leash at a street corner, I could be certain which little old lady would soon appear at the other end of that leash... Across from the Volks one evening when I was more reckless than usual, I'd pushed open the door of the Hôtel du Printemps and I tugged at the owner's heartstrings so successfully as I told him my story that he'd given me permission to take a shower there once a week... On a nearby street I'd got to know a bookstore owner and after just a few visits, guessing that I was poor, she'd urged me to take books away to look at them more closely at home; her name was Marianne, she was a kind of compromise between Jack and my little sister, and her eyes were the same blue as Mistassini's: a blue so bright that I always wanted to ask her if they shone at night like the eyes of cats.

On boulevard de Picpus, not on the pavement where the Volks was parked but on the road that went in the opposite direction, there was a woman of indeterminate age who had an antiques store and whom I'd nicknamed very impudently "the mummy." I would see her just before noon when I went out to buy *L'Équipe*. She would get some fresh air standing in the entrance to her store, with one hand gripping the door frame, and she would greet me with a nod and a kind word. Her curly hair was an indefinable colour, something between grey and pink, like the light on the renovated façades of old buildings, and it extended to her rumpled raincoat and even to the elastic bandages wrapped around her legs, which must have been covered with varicose veins. At night, one or two lamps in her store stayed on, and when I came home late I seemed to spot the woman of indeterminate age sitting in a velvet armchair, very erect and motionless, frozen for eternity in the midst of buffets, chaises longues, nesting tables, carafes, china, and lithographs.

Another little thing that I liked: at moments of calm I was sometimes lucky enough to hear from a nearby alleyway the voice of a town crier, slightly husky and high-pitched, which seemed to announce some mobile profession, but in terms that I couldn't quite grasp. When I got closer one day, I saw a man pushing a cart fitted out with various grindstones; he was crying "Grinder! Knives, scissors," but over time, I suppose, the words had got nicked like the tools he repaired.

All around me I kept seeing reasons to be happy. But I had to face facts: the traffic noise was unbearable. Though not very wide, the boulevard had two traffic lanes and the flood of cars which intensified as of seven a.m. had become even noisier because of a bus line connecting the Château de Vincennes with the Porte de Clignancourt.

The earplugs I used for work were either the Quies brand or some inflatable foam balls, which were more effective but which irritated the auditory canal. At night, however, nothing could protect me from the roar of motorcycles zooming towards the *boulevard périphérique*.

One morning, with my nerves on edge from another sleepless night, I decided to look for a quieter spot. After studying the map of the 12th arrondissement, I realized that I'd have to go to the Bois de Vincennes: it was nearby, so why hadn't I thought of it before?

The map was within reach on the passenger seat when I started the Volks; fortunately the motor ran smoothly and the brakes hadn't seized. Confident, I drove along the Cours de Vincennes, crossed the *périphérique*, turned right, and soon was on rue Chaussée-de-l'Étang, a kind of ring road that veered to the left as it followed the edge of the woods.

I was driving slowly because everything around me was beautiful. On one side were some old buildings lined up tidily behind heavy black metal gates, and on the other, some tall, broad-leaved trees between which appeared in sunny clearings a merry-go-round, some *pétanque* courts, a puppet theatre. A hundred metres or so along, the slope dropped suddenly to form a broad basin of greenery with a lake in the middle. On my right was a side street; it was one-way in the opposite direction so I backed onto it and parked the Volks in the first spot I found.

From there I had a view of the trees and the lake below; according to my map it was Saint-Mandé Lake. I got out of the vehicle to check the surrounding area. After crossing the ring road that had brought me here, I stopped for a moment at the top of a staircase that went down to the lake. I was surprised at the size and diversity of the trees. There were chestnuts, plane trees, acacias, oaks, several kinds of poplar, and a bald cypress that I took at first for a cedar.

The staircase brought me to the lake and I saw in the middle of it a small island with flowerbeds and stands of trees and, in particular, some willows that bowed their heads to let their long leafy boughs trail into the water.

The lake was really very small. It took five minutes to circle it following a dirt road. It was nothing like the lakes at home. Nothing like the one — though it was modest — where my sister and I

fished for trout when we were children. Nothing like the far bigger
lakes Mégantic and Memphremagog that the family Buick drove
around, purring, en route to our American vacations. Nor was it
anything like the lakes farther north, nearly at the ends of the roads,
whose names sang like the wind in the heads of the spruces: lakes
Waswanipi, Matagami, Peribonka, Chibougamau. And absolutely
nothing like the true Great Lakes of which it was impossible to see
the other shore, even in the cold, pure light of autumn, nor like the
countless lakes that spangle the map of Nouveau-Québec, north of
Hudson Bay, in the territories reserved for Indians and Inuit, that
whites can only reach by hydroplane.

Just as I was about to climb back up the stairs, I had an attack
of homesickness. To avoid giving in to it, I tried to look more
objectively at Saint-Mandé Lake and its surroundings. I noticed
carefully pruned trees, clipped lawns, cleared undergrowth, silent
and contemplative anglers, families of ducks and one lone swan: all
that made up a landscape whose various components were where
they belonged and in good order, and harmony was omnipresent.
Harmony, I told myself on my way back up the stairs, that was
the word which characterized most of the public or private places
I'd seen since arriving in France.

In my little house on wheels, I'd put water on to boil for coffee
and started to work on my translations when another word sprang
to mind, one that seemed to fit what I'd observed so far: the word
tradition. Right away, I laughed at myself, thinking that I was naively
discovering what everyone before me had already noted. While I
was making coffee I had another attack of homesickness: it was
very brief, and my pleasure at being in a setting of greenery and
water soon regained the upper hand.

The rue du Lac, to which I'd transported my home, was close to
stores and the Saint-Mandé-Tourelle Métro station, but it wasn't

very noisy. In the surrounding tranquillity that morning, after I'd inspected the neighbourhood, I was able to work as well as I did in Jack's bookstore in Quebec City. I rejoiced at the thought of experiencing an altogether quiet night for the first time in ages.

Two-fifteen a.m.: that was the time I saw on the dashboard of the Volks after I was wakened by the sound of a car. I got back in bed and it was hard to fall asleep. Nearly right away or so it seemed, another car yanked me from my sleep. This time, through the window in the sliding door I had time to see that the car was going very slowly with its sidelights on, and that it was being driven by a man accompanied by another person.

Just before daybreak, when I was wakened for the third time, I heard a car park on the other side of the street, across from the Volks. I stuck my nose out the window and in the faint light of dawn the movements that I made out inside the car, where one silhouette was bending across the other, told me what was going on: I had parked in a spot where the girls who paced the Cours de Vincennes at night were driven by the clients whom they relieved of the weight of their misery and their wallets.

This discovery made me smile and reassured me somewhat, because for a moment I'd been afraid that it was police in an unmarked car, or local residents annoyed at losing their parking spaces. On the other hand, as far as my search for peace and quiet was concerned, my troubles were far from over.

15

The Closerie des Lilas

"When you appear before some man of authority, remember that there is another who looks down from above on what passes here, and that it is him whom you must please rather than this man." That was the remark by Epictetus that I repeated to myself for reassurance as the Métro was taking me towards Montparnasse.

My concern had a precise cause, it even had a name and a face. The name was Philippe Rollers. As for the face, it was familiar to me, I'd seen it several times in newspapers and magazines and on TV shows that I'd watched against my better judgment when I was staying with Jack's friends.

It was not on my own initiative that I was going to see the man, but because Jack had asked me just before I boarded the plane in Quebec City: "Would you please *forget* my new novel at the Closerie des Lilas and bring it to the attention of the literary luminary Philippe Rollers?" That's what he asked me to do. He had added, "only if the opportunity arises," and those words, which were nothing more than a polite phrase, had served as a pretext ever since my arrival for not accomplishing my mission. Actually I knew perfectly well that the "opportunity" would never "arise" and my feeling of guilt had grown day by day.

I got off at the Luxembourg station. First I made a detour to the Librairie du Québec at 30 rue Gay-Lussac, where I bought Jack's book. The saleswoman had gentle eyes, a familiar style, and a lilting accent similar to mine. And from the basement came a song by Félix Leclerc that Jack was in the habit of singing to exercise his memory: each word resonated in my head a fraction of a second before I heard it, and it was as if old Jack himself had come to cheer me on. Half-confident and half-anxious, I set off again. Turning my back on the Jardin du Luxembourg, I started up boulevard Saint-Michel.

For once, the sky was uniformly blue. I forced myself to slow down because I hadn't yet thought up the ruse that would ensure that Jack's novel would end up in the hands of Philippe Rollers, an habitué of the Closerie, and make the famous Parisian writer feel an urge to read the first sentence — all that while I watched him to see his reactions as he read it.

I had learned of the existence of the Closerie des Lilas when I read *A Moveable Feast*. The restaurant, which stands at the corner of boulevard du Montparnasse and avenue de l'Observatoire, had been popular with artists and writers during the period between the wars. Hemingway could often be seen there, after he had moved nearby, to 113 rue Notre-Dame-des-Champs; he would sit on the terrace, or inside in winter, to write his short stories or to meet friends such as the poets Blaise Cendrars and Ezra Pound.

On the other hand, I knew nothing very specific about Philippe

Rollers. I didn't know his books, all I'd read was an article in *Le Monde* that dealt with style. I'd seen him on TV a couple of times and often heard him on the radio, on France-Culture, in my Volks: I couldn't see what people liked about him, except that he was very learned and quick-witted and he talked at the speed of a machine gun.

During literary programs on TV, I much preferred Sagan or Modiano, both of them rather pathetic, she because she muttered incomprehensibly, he because he never finished his sentences, there was fog in his eyes, and he seemed lost, like the ghosts that haunted his novels.

Even though he was wary of stars, Jack admired Rollers. He liked his ideas about literature and life and admired the detachment he could sense in all his books.

Deep in thought, I walked past the Closerie without noticing. I retraced my steps but, as I still hadn't drawn up a plan of action, I didn't dare to stop. I went back and forth with Jack's book several times and since it was at the bottom of my knapsack, it bumped my shoulder with every step I took. Aside from the arch-shaped entrance on boulevard du Montparnasse, the restaurant was completely surrounded by an opaque hedge of greenery and it was impossible to see if there were people on the terrace.

After ten minutes, afraid that my pacing back and forth would seem suspect, I decided to go inside: after all, the worst that could happen would be that I'd have a drink and leave without having placed the book where the famous writer would see it. As I got closer, I saw the Closerie's neon sign in an upstairs window. The sign was of course lilac-coloured, but I was so agitated that it wasn't till I was seated on the terrace that I made the connection with the restaurant's name. How could anyone be so dim-witted? I was still smiling at it when a waiter came to ask what I wanted.

"The same thing as Monsieur Rollers," I replied, amazed at my sudden boldness.

"He isn't here!" said the waiter curtly.

"Yes he is, he just arrived!"

The waiter turned around and looked at a corner of the terrace. It was only a quick glance but I was sure that his eyes had lit on the most distant table, an unoccupied one in a corner near the hedge of greenery. Then gave me a disapproving look. To present a bold front, I took Jack's book from my knapsack as slowly as I could and set it down in front of me in its plastic bag which showed the bookstore's slogan: "A Corner of Quebec in the Heart of Paris."

"You got me!" declared the waiter.

"Pardon?" I asked innocently.

"You wanted to know where Philippe Rollers' table was, didn't you?"

"That's right. I'm sorry... Are you angry?"

"Not really. You're Québécois?"

"Yes."

"A *cunning* Québécois from what I can see." He'd used the Québécois term *ratoureux*.

"Oh ... do you know Quebec?"

"No, but my roommate worked there for ten years, so there are some Québécois books in the apartment: novels, poetry, a dictionary... Hang on, I'll be right back."

A couple had just arrived. American tourists: a tall blonde in sunglasses and a well-dressed young man; both had an aristocratic manner and seeing them, it was hard not to think about Zelda and Scott Fitzgerald. The waiter put them at a table not far from the entrance, brought them martinis or something of the sort, then came back to me.

"What was I saying?"

"You were saying there are Québécois books in your bookcase."

"Ah, yes..."

"Do you know this one?" I asked, taking the novel from the plastic bag. The waiter picked it up and after a quick look at the cover, he turned it over to read the blurb. It was as if it was burning his fingers because he flipped it over and read aloud the author's name: "Jack Waterman."

"No, I don't know this one," he said.

"He's my father," I said.

The words had come out by themselves, it was the second time I'd made this slip, and I wasn't proud of myself.

"Is it any good?" asked the waiter.

"That's just it," I said, "there's a small problem..."

"What kind?"

"My father would like to know how a man like Philippe Rollers would react if he discovered this book *by chance* and started to read the first page."

"What do the critics say?"

"The reviews are fairly good, but the author, I mean my father, would like to have the opinion of a Paris intellectual. He has developed a theory about the first sentence. In his opinion, the first sentence should be like an open window, a light in the darkness or the smile of an unknown woman — something so attractive and seductive that you can't resist the urge to go on reading. And he wants me to stay here and check that everything's going as expected, do you understand?"

"Absolutely."

"His first sentence is supposed to be irresistible. Would you like to see for yourself?"

"No, don't bother, I'm not a member of the literati."

"I insist," I say, holding out the book open to the first page. In fact his opinion didn't matter: I just wanted him to feel involved and to offer me his help.

"Hmmm!" he said. "It looks pretty good... How will you arrange to make Monsieur Rollers pick up the book? Have you any ideas?"

"No, not one," I said, putting it back in the plastic bag. "You?"

"Me?" said the waiter. "Just a minute please..." He went to the American tourists near the door: the man had held up a finger to mime writing something on his hand. The waiter gave him the bill, the man paid, the waiter came back. "What you want," he said, "is for me to give Monsieur Rollers the book, right?"

"I didn't have the nerve to ask you," I said, trying to look as humble as possible. "I'd intended to put the book on his chair, so it would look as if someone had left it behind, but first of all I don't know when he gets here..."

"It's not even sure that he'll come!"

"And then he could also pick up the book and put it on the table without looking at it, out of discretion or something like that... Does he usually bring something to read?"

"Yes, he reads *Le Monde*."

"And he should be here soon?"

The waiter looked at his watch.

"He should be here by now," he said, "but he doesn't come every day. Ah! I think I've got an idea... I'll put the book on his chair and if you see that he's not opening it, let me know discreetly and I'll go up to him and say it's by an author who's not too well known but who's well regarded in the United States..."

"And you'll add, 'in university circles,' he'll be even more impressed!"

"All right. Now what can I bring you?"

"Scotch and soda."

It wasn't my usual drink, it was what Hemingway drank with Fitzgerald, according to *A Moveable Feast*. They would drink several in a row, then Fitzgerald's face would suddenly look waxen and he would pass out.

"Good choice," said the waiter, "that's what Monsieur Rollers drinks."

"I just thought of something," I said. "Would it be better to leave the book in its plastic bag or what?"

"No!" he snapped, suddenly irritated. "You have to take it out! Otherwise, when he sees the word 'Québec' on the bag I guarantee that Monsieur Rollers won't want to look inside."

"Why? Aren't Paris intellectuals interested in Québec literature?"

"I didn't say that!"

He protested vehemently, then left the terrace and looked around outside.

"Monsieur Rollers isn't there," he whispered as he walked past my table. He went inside and came back with a scotch and soda, serving it to me without a word. I took a small sip, then left the terrace as well to look around. I turned the corner and as I walked behind the verdigris statue of Maréchal Ney, I took a few steps along the avenue de l'Observatoire. All at once I spotted the writer going along the sidewalk on inline skates, hands in his pockets, elegant and nearly floating, with his cigarette holder between his lips and a light scarf drifting down his back.

I raced back as fast as I could.

"He's on his way!" I called out to the waiter. Without wasting a second, he picked up Jack's book and tossed it onto Rollers's chair. Then he rushed inside and I followed him because my heart was racing and I couldn't conceal my nervousness. I went to the bathroom and when I came back, spotting a copy of *L'Équipe* on the bar where the waiter was leaning across from the barman, I asked permission to take it. The barman nodded and the waiter gave me an encouraging smile.

With the paper under my arm, I assumed an aloof manner and went back to my seat on the terrace. I'd foolishly left behind the bag on the table next to my drink, so I quickly stuffed it into my knapsack. Philippe Rollers was already sitting at the table that was reserved for him in the corner, near the hedge. He had Jack's novel in front of him.

The waiter arrived and greeted him respectfully.

"Your usual, monsieur?"

"Please."

Monsieur Rollers, who had replaced his skates with sandals, opened *Le Monde* and smiled as he looked at the Plantu cartoon. From where I was sitting I could simply look up and see his face. His greying hair, cut in bangs on his forehead, would have made him look like a monk if it weren't for the cigarette holder between his teeth. When the waiter brought his drink I opened my paper and behind that shelter, which I could shift as I wished, I watched what was going on.

While trying not to block my view, the waiter was explaining something to Monsieur Rollers, who nodded and kept on reading *Le Monde*.

Finally, he put down his paper and picked up Jack's novel. He took a brief look at the cover, a longer look at the blurb, and set it back down on the table. He had already picked up his newspaper when the waiter leaned over and whispered something in his ear. I had lowered my own paper few centimetres, just enough so I could watch the scene closely. I can't swear to it, but it seemed to me that the writer looked in my direction. Then he picked up Jack's book again and opened it to the first page.

Despite all my efforts my newspaper was shaking as if I had Parkinson's disease. As he read, Monsieur Rollers began to draw on his cigarette with a kind of hunger that seemed to me to bode well and I felt somewhat reassured. He read the entire first page, then turned it and glanced at a few lines on the other side. A little smile brightened his face when he put down the book and it seemed to me that Jack had won his bet.

I took a long gulp of scotch and soda. As he passed my table, the waiter gave me a wink of complicity, then went back inside and I hastened to go in and thank him. He claimed it was nothing and said he was very glad to have been of service to someone from Quebec. As he shook my hand though he had the awkward and self-conscious look of someone who isn't telling the whole truth; at the time I didn't pay attention to that detail.

I went back to the terrace. It was late and I was preparing to finish my drink without wasting time when Rollers picked up Jack's book and abruptly got to his feet. I nearly had a fit when I realized that he was coming towards me.

He set the book down on my table.

I pretended to be totally absorbed in *L'Équipe*. It was Wimbledon time and Pete Sampras, one of my great idols, had just won the tournament for the sixth time, beating Björn Borg's record. The account of the final, in which he'd played André Agassi, was fascinating: the reporter claimed that no one in the entire history of tennis had played better on grass than Sampras had played that day. Agassi, defeated in three consecutive sets, had said of his opponent that he "walked on water," and Sampras himself had remarked: "I was in the zone." Those last word hadn't been translated and while I tried mentally to ignore the presence of Philippe Rollers next to my table, I was trying desperately to come up with the best translation, hesitating between *J'étais sur un nuage* and another expression that had the virtue of simplicity: *Je planais*.

"I'm returning your book," said Monsieur Rollers calmly.

"Excuse me?" I said, as if I were very surprised to see him.

"This book belongs to you, doesn't it?"

"Yes, but..."

"You wanted to know how I would react when I read the beginning?"

"Umm..."

"Does my reaction please you?"

I folded my newspaper and looked up at him. His teeth were clenched around his eternal cigarette holder, but there was no sign of hostility on his face.

"How could you tell?" I asked.

"It was easy, I'd seen *Québec* on the bag that was on your table when I got here," he said. "And you were reading *L'Équipe*: that's a morning paper so I thought to myself that you weren't French."

"Well done," I said, even though I actually thought that his last argument didn't hold water.

"I don't deserve any credit: people are always sticking books under my nose to see my reaction. I have a certain experience if I may say so."

"My sincere apologies!"

"No harm done," he said, then suddenly turned and walked away. Just as he was sitting down he came to a halt like Inspector Colombo, then returned to me. "I've forgotten one small detail," he said. "The book starts off very well!"

I drained my scotch and soda in one gulp and, unaccustomed to that kind of drink, I went back to the minibus smiling and saying *bonjour* to everyone like a zouave.

16

A Letter With No End

Three a.m. and I had hardly slept. Even with earplugs I'd been wakened by car noise: the girls on the Cours de Vincennes worked all night. On top of that, a disreputable-looking individual had tried to look inside the Volks with a flashlight: he may have been a pimp who wanted to eliminate the competition.

Jack had told me about a defence system that he'd used when he travelled diagonally across America to California. When he spent the night in a seedy part of cities like Detroit or Chicago, he stuck a sign reading "Beware of the Dog!" on the back window; and if he heard suspect sounds around the vehicle, he played a tape of the fierce barking of a German shepherd.

In the Bois de Vincennes there was no reason to fear for my life. It was at most my own comfort that was threatened, but as I'd spent several sleepless nights I'd run out of patience. Around half-past three, ignoring the Stoic precepts of Epictetus, I got behind the wheel of the minibus, barefoot and wearing only the T-shirt I used as pyjamas, and headed back to the 12th arrondissement.

Obliged to take a long detour because of the one-way streets, I lost my way in the small streets and the cul-de-sacs. By chance, just as I began to despair of finding my way again, I came to an avenue that brought me to the Château de Vincennes. According to my map I just had to go left, towards the city centre whose faint lights I could already see. After I'd found a bridge that crossed the *périphérique*, I was surprised to note that I was already on the Cours de Vincennes. Though it was the middle of the night there was a nearly uninterrupted parade of cars and motorcycles and there were lights on all over. My impatience gradually dissolved. I turned on the heat in the Volks to warm my feet. And, before I started to look for a new parking space, I gave myself the luxury of circling three times the spotlit monument under the tall plane trees, in the centre of the Place de la Nation.

After that I drove down the boulevard de Picpus. I went past the spot where I'd parked before, then up a one-way street whose name I liked because it stirred images in my head: rue du Rendez-Vous. It was so peaceful at that hour that when I arrived at the top, I parked on the left in the first available spot. Before I lay down again to try to get a few hours' sleep, I looked around the Volks. Everything that I could see, or almost, was familiar: the Franprix market, the seamstress, the bakery, the bistro Le Chalet, Marianne's bookstore, and King Philippe Auguste at the summit of his stone column.

A few days later, Françoise, my neighbourhood mail-carrier, dropped an envelope onto the passenger seat and I recognized Mistassini's handwriting. I opened it quickly. My sister said that she was writing me a "letter with no end" and that when I'd finished it, I would understand what she meant.

She had introduced some innovations to *la librairie du vieux* as we called it affectionately, thinking of both Vieux-Québec and old Jack. For instance, she'd changed the way the books were placed on the shelves. She had noticed that as readers moved towards the shelves, they disliked having to tip their heads to one side to read the title and the author's name, and that they were more willing to pick up books that had been removed from their ranks and placed face-out. To choose these books, which sold well, she had set up a system of rotation based on the best-seller list, but that started with the ones at the bottom.

She had also made a summer window display that she was quite pleased with. Jack had told her she could feature not the practical books and light novels that reviewers recommend that you "put in your beach bag," but rather philosophy books, serious studies, and difficult novels, reckoning that during their vacations, when they were free of work constraints and the mindlessness of TV, people were better prepared to read important books that they'd set aside during the year.

Jack came every day to lend a hand, despite the fact that he'd started to translate a young English-Canadian novelist. When he was feeling well, he would even take the time to show her some little tricks of the trade... How to reply to a lady who called to ask if they had the novel of which she'd seen the film adaptation on TV and the adaptation didn't have the same title as the novel and the lady felt obliged to recount the entire story of the film... How to turn her head at the right moment to give students and readers who were poor time to steal the books piled up next to the door for that purpose ... How to arrange things so that a customer who'd come to buy the latest bestseller by Stephen King would leave with the first novel by a Quebec writer who, though unknown, already had his own style.

She hadn't wanted to say it right away, but Jack was not doing well. I felt a pang when I saw those few words in my vehicle on rue du Rendez-Vous. In fact when I was reading the letter two questions kept running around in my head: had Jack's condition got worse and had my little sister found someone?

Mist had trouble being specific about what was wrong in his behaviour. Thanks to his efforts to recall the lyrics of old songs, his memory didn't seem to have diminished. What's more, he very much enjoyed his new work as a literary translator.

She had the impression, however, that his contact with reality was becoming intermittent and she gave as an example a theory that he'd constructed. From looking into the novel that he was translating, slowly and cautiously, Jack had had what he called a "revelation": a book could be compared to a city. Everything that was white in a book — margins, paragraph indentations, and spaces at the ends of chapters — gave the reader a chance to rest and played the same role as the benches, gardens, and parks in a city. Everything that was black — words, lines, and paragraphs — corresponded to the houses, streets, and neighbourhoods. And the white space in the middle, where the paper was folded, was obviously like a river that divided the city in two.

While it was simplistic and far-fetched, this theory didn't suggest to Mist any worsening of his "Eisenhower's disease." Which was my opinion too, but something more disturbing had happened.

One Saturday at the end of the day, the bookstore had gradually emptied of customers — more numerous because of the Summer Festival — until the only one left was a girl who leaned on the counter, her arms crossed on a notebook. She was just skin and bones, her face was half-hidden by a shock of hair, and she had on a long dress with puffed sleeves and two layers of frills and flounces. She could have stepped out of a novel by the Brontë sisters.

Thinking that she'd brought a manuscript, Mist had suggested that she place it on one of the shelves. Then the girl explained that it was a thesis she was writing about Jack's novels. She had come to ask if he would answer a few questions.

Stretched out in his reclining chair with his feet on the desk, Jack was smoking a cigarette in silence. He acted as if he hadn't heard a thing. The girl clutched her notebook nervously and seemed about to run away. To restore her confidence, Mist had asked her about the themes that she was tackling in her work. It was an M.A. thesis dealing with intertextuality and post-modernism. The girl's explanations had been precise and easy to understand, but seeing no reaction from Jack, she started to walk to the door. Mist had taken her by the hand then and led her to the office.

Finally, Jack had agreed to answer her questions. After ten minutes or so however his replies had become evasive and more and more brief. When Mist left them to make coffee in the Parenthesis, he joined her and told her about his suspicions: the girl was an emissary of the Hôtel-Dieu; using the pretext of university courses, she had been charged with checking to see if he had remembered every single detail of what happened in his novels.

Back in the store where Mist had served the coffee, his answers to the girl's questions had become monosyllabic. Finally she asked him if she'd made a mistake, been indiscreet, or done something wrong. Jack had uttered a few obscure remarks, including, "Please, leave the old writers alone." The young girl had gone away in tears, leaving her notebook behind on the counter. Mist had caught up with the girl on rue Saint-Jean and when she gave back her thesis, tried to console her by explaining that Jack was going through a bad period.

In the Volks, in Paris, my heart was with Mist and I was as upset as she was. I could see her now rushing back to the bookstore where Jack was waiting for her, devastated by the feeling that he'd been unnecessarily aggressive. She told him that he mustn't worry because in any event, his memory hadn't failed. To reassure him, she made him sing one of the songs that he'd learned by heart. He passed the test but as his doubts had not been completely erased, she promised to learn one of the songs herself — *Le Petit Bonheur* — and she promised to find among his friends someone for each of the other songs in his repertory. That way, if his memory should fail there would always be someone around to whisper the forgotten words. She'd got the idea while reading *Fahrenheit 451*, by Ray Bradbury.

Since then, Jack had been calling Mist "Petit Bonheur" or little happiness. There hadn't been another incident. She'd signed up for a course in self defence because she was tired of being bothered when she came home late at night. She had left her apartment in Limoilou and was staying at the bookstore, or sometimes, when he needed help, at Jack's place. Charabia, the black cat, had put on weight and now went out at night; he'd also expanded his repertoire of meows.

Wondering anxiously if there were now new ties between Jack and my little sister, I first sped through, then read slowly the tender words with which she told me that I mustn't interrupt my trip, but that she missed me. My heart turned upside down when she talked about the days we'd spent working in the bookstore side by side, the meals we'd eaten together in the Parenthesis, the evenings when we were happy to read, to trade books, then to lean against one another and doze, most of the time hardly daring to move.

When she reached that point in her letter, Mist had to stop because she couldn't find the appropriate words for the rest. That was why she'd said at the beginning that she was writing "a letter with no end."

17

The Women's Bus

Shortly after I arrived in Paris, I had realized one of my dreams: to attend the Roland-Garros Tournament in the Bois de Boulogne, where Pete Sampras, my favourite tennis player, was hoping to take away the only trophy still missing from his incomparable list of prizes.

Sampras seemed to play tennis for aesthetic reasons. His moves were so fluid, so well coordinated that he was able to hit the ball more powerfully and more precisely than his opponents, while expending less effort. I thought his game was elegant and sober, and it was pleasant to think that those were the very words Jack used to define the kind of writing he liked. The quality of Sampras's play was, however, not so fine on clay, where he had to slide at the very moment when he hit the ball. At Roland-Garros that year, which seemed to be the last chance for a player of his age, I'd had to acknowledge that he'd made no progress on that surface: he'd lost the quarter finals. Clay was not his natural element.

At the same time I had taken a brief jaunt outside Paris to attend the 24 Hours of Le Mans. I wanted to see the great Henri Pescarolo. As he'd become known during endurance races rather than at the wheel of a Formula One, he didn't have the reputation of drivers like Prost, Schumacher or Senna, or even older ones like Fangio, Moss, or Clark. For racing journalists and people in the field, however, he was quite simply a master.

Now that he was team captain, Pescarolo had a chance of winning the 24 Hours with a new car, the *Courage*. And so I got onto the highway to Le Mans and after leaving the Volks in the big parking lot where I could go now and then for a bite to eat and to take a rest, I spent my time in the stands, enjoying the sight of the prototypes and sports cars as they travelled the circuit, first under the harsh light of the sun, then at night with their garlands of lights like Christmas tree decorations, and after that in the dangerous early morning fog. Finally, when the checkered flag was brought down, Pescarolo's *Courage*, which had suffered some mechanical problems, didn't even cross the finish line.

Two weeks later, that disappointment didn't stop me from going to the Magny-Cours circuit in the Nièvre to see how Jacques Villeneuve, the Québécois Formula One driver, would do in France's Grand Prix. After winning the World Championship, he had helped to form a new stable: that difficult endeavour was taking a long time to bear fruit but in my heart, at every new race, I held onto the insane hope that his slightly clumsy one-seater would let him finish in front. I spent the whole weekend at Magny-Cours then, attending the practice and the race. The results had been disappointing: the best that Villeneuve could do was to place fourth.

On the way home I got stuck in traffic jams that lasted all the way to the junction with the highway at Auxerre, then formed again as I approached Paris. When at last I found a parking place at the top of rue du Rendez-Vous it was late, my back ached, my head was full of the roar of engines, and I was grappling with the disheartening notion that my heroes in the world of sports were on their way out. I gulped some green vegetable soup, then I hesitated between pasta and canned tuna with rice. Uncomfortable because of the heat from the gas stove, I lay down on the back seat; drew the curtains and took off my jeans.

I was wakened in the middle of the night by the characteristic clicking of high heels on the sidewalk. When it came level with the Volks, the click-clack seemed to hesitate briefly, then moved on. I wasn't really worried — a thief wouldn't have made so much noise — but I nonetheless sat up and listened, out of curiosity. The person had probably turned the corner of boulevard de Picpus, because now I couldn't hear anything. Lying down on the seat again, I covered the lower part of my body with a cotton sheet.

No sooner had I dozed off, it seemed to me, than I heard again the clicking of heels on the sidewalk. As they had earlier, the steps were coming from the bottom of the street, but this time they stopped in front of the Volks. Very irritated, I pulled the sheet over my head in case the person should decide to look through the windshield and tried hard not to stir. I slowed down my breathing so that the sheet wouldn't move.

The door on the driver's side opened without the slightest resistance, which amazed me because it seemed to me that I'd locked it before I lay down again. The smell of cheap perfume spread through the minibus and I heard a strange voice: "I know you're in there under the sheet, and your heart is racing."

The voice was weird, at once soft and rasping. The person was right about my heart: it was pounding as if I'd run a hundred metres in ten seconds. But how had this person got inside so easily? Why the interest in my heart? What about that voice, which reminded me of Marlene Dietrich, one of Jack's favourite singers?

I sat up cross-legged on the back seat, keeping the sheet around my hips and over my legs. I had nothing on underneath.

"Excuse me for waking you in the middle of the night," said the person.

"That's quite all right," I said in an offhand manner that suggested I entertained people every night and that this new arrival hadn't disturbed me in the least.

The person sat sideways on the seat, back against the door, legs stretched out on the passenger seat, and I heard shoes drop onto the floor of the Volks. I craned my neck so I could get a look at the legs and feet. The individual had on a leather mini and dark tights torn at the knee; the legs were long and slim with muscular calves and rather narrow feet around the same length as mine. This brief examination couldn't help me decide if I was dealing with a woman or a transvestite; the face, which was rather young and lightly made-up, could belong to either sex.

"What's the verdict?" asked the person.

"There's no verdict," I replied.

"Does that bother you?"

"It doesn't make the *slightest* difference!"

For some strange reason I felt a need to make the person believe that the question of sex didn't matter to me in the least. It didn't work, as far as I could tell, but at least the person seemed to relax.

"Feels good to rest your legs," said the person.

"Do you do a lot of walking?" I asked stupidly.

"It's a good thing I do! Otherwise the cops would be there... We used to have the Women's Bus: that was in the good old days. It was a place where we could take a break at any hour of the night. Do you remember?"

"No, I wasn't in Paris. I was in Quebec."

"Are you Canadian?"

"No I'm not Canadian! I'm QUÉBÉCOIS!!!"

I was sick and tired of repeating that time and again, so I muttered between my teeth but loud enough to be heard: "Québécois, *tabarnak!*"

"I like the last syllable in *tabarnak*," said the person. "Like the sound of a whip. You know, that reminds me of a book by Jack London that's set up north in Quebec... A story about dog sleds and the sound of whips cracking above the dog teams... I've forgotten the title."

"*White Fang*," I said, "but the story isn't set in Quebec, it's in the Yukon! Which is in the west, at the other end of Canada!"

"It's all the same to me."

"Whatever makes you happy... So what was this Women's Bus?"

"A red double-decker, bought in London, that was parked on the Cours de Vincennes. It was there every night and it was a shelter for the girls who wanted to take a breather, get new needles or condoms, or have a coffee, talk with someone or receive first aid. Sometimes the girls are attacked..."

"Our cities are more and more violent," I said in a sententious tone that was new to me.

"That's what everybody thinks," she said.

"And it isn't true?"

"Depends. In the Women's Bus there were always some books lying around. One night I read the letters Stendahl had written to his sister, Pauline. Not all of them, just the first ones written during the 1800s. Stendahl was travelling at the time and he wrote to his sister, who'd stayed in Grenoble, their native city. He wanted to share with her everything he was learning on his travels. For instance he told her that in Paris, if you counted the murders, the suicides, and the victims of duels, it added up to forty deaths per day: that's a lot more than today, isn't it?"

"You're right," I said, "especially because at the turn of the 19th century the population of Paris was certainly smaller."

"It was eight hundred thousand... Say, have you got anything to drink?"

This person's knowledge and precise explanations were very impressive. I wished I had something luxurious to offer: *cognac à l'orange, mirabelle, crème de cassis...* Alas! All I had was some mediocre muscat that wasn't even cold.

"Muscat? That's perfect!"

I was trying to find the bottle and glasses, which was difficult because I had to open the doors of the cupboard under the gas burner and at the same time keep the sheet around my waist. My guest told me about having a philosopher as a client one day. He had said that society was advancing towards peace and justice, "with the majestic but inexorable slowness of a glacier."

I was more and more impressed, but it occurred to me that the person might be a sociologist disguised as a streetwalker for the purpose of a scientific study. Venturing a glance in the person's direction, I realized that I was wrong: on a pocket mirror were two lines of white powder and in the individual's hand, a piece of a straw.

"Want some?"

"No thanks," I said, "it's a little early for me. Have you got some grass by any chance?"

"Sorry."

Once the coke was snorted, my new acquaintance held out a hand.

"My name is Dominique."

"Mine's Jimmy."

The two biggest drug addicts in the 12th arrondissement shook hands. Neither the first name, which could be that of either a man or a woman, nor the handshake, which was firm but not vigorous, gave any clues about the person's sex.

I poured the muscat and held out a glass.

"Thanks," said my drinking buddy and then, "you have an English name?"

"It's because of Jim Clark, a racing driver who killed himself some time before I was born. My father was a big fan of his."

"And that's why you live in a car?"

After draining the glass in two gulps, the person's head was turned towards me. Though the face was backlit by a street lamp, I sensed that the person was making eyes at me. They didn't have the tenderness of Mistassini's blue eyes: they were darker and a little murky. My excitement was so great though that as I tried to answer this last question, I found myself once again really over-doing it.

I said that I lived in a minibus in the middle of the city because coming from America as I did, ever since I was a child I couldn't stop paying heed to the call of the highways that disappeared into the mountains at the end of the horizon.

The person was still looking, but it seemed to me that the eyes now held a bit of curiosity or amusement mixed with the tenderness. I went on with my explanations, inventing as I went along, saying whatever popped into my head. I wonder where it all came from.

I declared that material success didn't interest me. I was a descendant of the hippies: I liked their mentality, except that I'd rejected all ideologies and all principles. I didn't want to change the world, it revolved without me and I had no hold over it. I didn't even have dreams, all I had left was a small flickering flame deep in my heart.

The person was silent for a few moments, then asked for half a glass of muscat and downed it in one gulp. Setting the glass on the dashboard beside the compass, my visitor stretched both arms and legs, murmuring with contentment. Suddenly, the right arm reached out and with a brisk, even virile movement, the cotton sheet that I'd managed to keep around my waist all this time was yanked away.

"There! Now I can see that little flame! Listen, I have to go back to work but I can do something to thank you for your hospitality. It's a Chinese trick that's not very well known, called 'The horse gallops while looking at flowers.' Just lie down. Interested?"

With legs folded under and leaning forward, my visitor prepared to join me on the back seat.

"Yes or no?"

"Thanks, but I prefer cybersex," I replied.

I said that for its shock value but it obviously didn't shock in the least. With a shrug the person left the Volks, giving me a friendly smile anyway. I listened to the footsteps: a right turn at the end of rue du Rendez-Vous would lead back to the Cours de Vincennes. While the clicking of heels died away in the night, I had to admit that I'd been a total idiot. I hadn't done any better than my idols, Sampras, Pescarolo, and Villeneuve.

18

Second Letter With No End

From a distance I thought I saw a ticket on the windshield of the Volks. As I got closer, carrying the croissants I'd just bought from the bakery at the top of the street, I was relieved to see that it was just a note jotted on a scrap of paper.

It was from Jack's friends. They'd noticed the minibus when they did their daily shopping at the Franprix and when they went to the big market on the Cours de Vincennes on Saturdays and Wednesdays. Somewhat surprised that I was still in Paris, they wanted to invite me for a meal, but they'd kept putting it off. Finally an opportunity had come up: they had a letter for me. I hadn't had mail for a while, because Françoise was away on her August vacation.

The TV was on when I arrived that evening, and they didn't turn it off when I came in or when we were having drinks or when we were eating. At dessert, they gave me the letter: it was from Mistassini. The writing on the envelope kept changing, slanting first to the left, then to the right, and I guessed that something serious was going on in Quebec. The body of the letter started in the same way as the one before: my little sister was taking advantage of the fact that she was alone in the bookstore to write me another "letter with no end." A few lines after that, the tone changed abruptly. Jack had been attacked by someone. I tried to figure out what exactly had happened, but it wasn't easy to concentrate with the constant chatter of the TV news, to which were added the comments of Jack's friends who were denouncing the poor quality of the reports; still, they didn't turn it off. For the time being then I let my gaze brush against Mistassini's words till the final sentences where, as in the first letter, there were words for me that were as soft as velvet. I closed my eyes the better to feel them.

"Bad news?" asked my worried hosts.

"No, no," I said, "everything's fine."

"Jack's not sick I hope?"

"No, he's fine."

They left it at that.

I put the letter back in the envelope. I was determined to leave Jack's friends and their noisy TV set, but it was already time for the movie. We could hear a fine bass voice singing, "*Do not forsake me O my darlin'/On this our wedding day.*" and on the screen unfolded the first images of a film that I liked a lot, *High Noon*. Gary Cooper was looking for people to fight a gang of outlaws whose leader was a deadly killer who would be arriving on the noon train; in the end, he would be all alone to confront death.

That loneliness could only make me think about old Jack and about the "little push" we'd talked about in Quebec one spring evening. At the end of the film, the theme song continued to echo in my head, punctuated by the whistle of the train. I got up and stretched to show that I needed to move. They did the same and then, expressing surprise at how quickly time flies, I turned down the one last drink they offered and left them with thanks for such an excellent meal and such a pleasant evening; I was once again the biggest liar in the 12th arrondissement.

Inside the Volks, I closed the curtains, then switched on the best lamp, the one with a fluorescent tube, and reread Mist's letter in the peace and quiet. My sister had a very special way of telling stories. She gave a mass of details as if she'd witnessed every event in the drama. Her narrative was very realistic and I could see quite effortlessly what she was describing. I was moved and swept away by the intensity of the story.

One evening Jack leaves the bookstore, saying that he feels like walking around in the city. The days are getting shorter, already the sky has a purple hue, but the air is still mild for the season. He has on a denim windbreaker and in the left-hand pocket is a note explaining what he was preparing to do.

He hangs around the Place d'Youville, asking questions of vagrants he's seen in the bookstore where they take shelter in bad weather. He is told that he has the best chance of finding what he wants in the Saint-Roch neighbourhood. So he boards the first bus that comes down the Côte d'Abraham and takes it to Place Jacques-Cartier. And there, walking where the spirit moves him because he hasn't been in this part of town for years, he spends half an hour roaming some streets: rue Saint-Joseph, rue Notre-Dame-des-Anges, rue Sainte-Hélène.

On the sidewalk outside a restaurant, he notices a girl who is leaning against a parking meter. She's very young, with red hair, pale complexion, short skirt, and a kind of jersey that leaves her stomach mostly bare. Her clothes and her far-too-conspicuously nonchalant attitude testify to the fact that despite appearances, she's hard at work.

"Fifty bucks," she says. "A special price because it's you."

"Hi!" he says. "Is your name Lola by any chance?"

"Who told you that?" she asks, laughing. "What's your pleasure: come with me or ask questions?"

"Go with you. If it's not too far..."

"Are you tired?"

"I'm old."

"Hang on, we'll do something about that."

She turns around and glances at one of the restaurant windows, then gestures discreetly. Jack looks in the same direction. Dazzled by the glint of the setting sun on the glass, he doesn't see anyone at the window, then suddenly he catches sight of a kind of signal: the flame of a lighter or a match. A few seconds after that a door slams next to the restaurant, then he sees a car drive out of a nearby alley. A collector's item: a metallic blue Firebird. It is parked along the sidewalk, in front of the meter that the girl is leaning against. The driver is a man with a shaven head.

It was obvious that Mist's story was about to get complicated. I took a break, long enough to fix myself a hot chocolate. When I went back to her letter, chewing on a heel of a baguette left over from breakfast, Jack asks the girl to wait a minute and gets into the Firebird next to the driver.

Instead of saying clearly what he wants, Jack expresses himself through gestures and allusions. The man with the shaven head doesn't understand and offers him all kinds of drugs and pills. Finally, Jack stretches out his arm as if to aim at something and the man bends over and takes a pistol from under the seat. It's a 22-calibre Beretta, a compact model, the kind that the girls

sometimes carry in their purses for protection. Jack has no trouble
hiding it in the pocket of his windbreaker where already there's a
letter of explanation. The man says that the weapon is loaded; he
shows Jack how it works and names the price. Jack gives him the
money, gets out of the car, and pays the girl as well. The Firebird
drives away.

"Are you coming?" asks the girl.

"Not right away. There's something urgent that I have to do."

"Then you don't owe me anything."

"I'll pay anyway."

"No!"

She tries to give him back the money. He won't take it, so she
stuffs it into the right-hand pocket of his windbreaker.

"Thanks," he says.

"If I were you," she says, patting his other pocket, "I wouldn't
use that."

"I'll think about it. Thanks, Lola."

"You say thanks but you mean to do it anyway..."

"I have no idea. Anyway, it's very kind of you to try. It warms my
heart."

"There's sadness in your eyes."

"That's life. Bye, now!"

"Bye!"

With a friendly gesture, as if to show him what he's missing, she
pulls her little skirt up by about a hand's width. Jack smiles, lights
two cigarettes, gives her one; and then, after a brief hesitation, he
walks on to the nearest bus stop.

Back in Upper Town, he passes through the Porte Saint-Jean and
after taking a few steps in the direction of his bookstore, changes
his mind and starts to make his way up rue d'Auteuil. The slope is
too steep for his tired legs. He stops at the terrace of a restaurant

close to the Jesuits' chapel and orders lemon pie and coffee. Now that he can feel in his pocket the object he has desired for some time, he pays close attention to everything he sees: the waitress sways as she walks and the motion of her hips makes the evening air move in a waltz; lights on the roofs of hotels merge with the first stars; the outlines of life become softer.

In the vehicle on rue du Rendez-Vous, even though I knew that the letter was going to take a tragic turn, I couldn't help smiling at the details Mist had chosen.

Because the waitress is taking a long time to bring his bill, Jack leaves the terrace and goes inside. As he's paying for his snack he notices a woman slumped on a chair in front of an empty glass. She raises her head. She's a little old lady with untidy grey hair.

"You want my picture?" she asks in a voice as rough as sandpaper.

"My apologies," says Jack.

"Aren't you the man that owns the bookstore?"

"Yes."

"So you can afford to buy me a beer."

"Gladly."

He gestures to the waitress who, with a courtesy that's nearly affectionate, brings the woman a beer. She takes a long gulp, wipes her lips with the back of her hand, then speaks to Jack.

"Don't you recognize me?"

"I'm losing my memory," he says sadly.

"In the old days I often used to go to the bookstore. Especially in winter on account of the stove, but in the summer too: you'd lend me books and I could read them outside right till sunset. The last one I read was by you... Are you still writing?"

"No," he says, and adds sotto voce: "In the past, my stories used to fall to wrack and ruin while I was trying to write them. Now I've become a ruin myself."

"When you mutter like that I can't understand a word."

He apologizes and says more clearly, "If it's not indiscreet, aren't you part of the group that occupies the Porte Saint-Louis? The group of ... what's it called?"

"That's my son," she says proudly. "His name is Johnny. You want to see him?"

"I've got business with him."

"They went to the Plains by the stairs that go down to the Dufferin Terrace. Usually they set up in the big kiosk, the one at the top of the stairs, but if you don't find them, the last thing you should do is worry: they'll find you!"

"Thank you, Madame."

"They left me here because I'm too old."

"And how do you handle old age?"

"I drink."

"That helps?"

"No. How about you, what do you do?"

"Actually that's why I want to see Johnny."

Leaving the restaurant, he climbs the steepest part of rue d'Auteuil, then goes up the steps of the Porte Dauphine and onto the path that pedestrians have opened along the top of the walls. It crosses the open space where pieces of cardboard, sleeping bags, empty bottles and syringes testify to a recent stay by Johnny's gang. Some distance away he arrives at the big park on the Plains. A grassy slope, then a paved road take him to the kiosk. No one is there. Tired, he lies down on a bench and falls asleep.

He's wakened by a sharp pain in his back. At first he thinks he's put his back out, but when a burst of light falls on his face he realizes that he's being attacked. He can feel a hard, pointed object in his back, an object that can only be Lola's pistol, because it's no longer in his windbreaker pocket.

All at once the pain stops and he hears an authoritarian voice ask,

"What're you looking for?"

"Could you stop pointing that light at me?" he asks.

The light goes out. Once his eyes are used to the dark, Jack can get a good look at the leader of the gang. Johnny is a tall, broad-shouldered man, but with his thick dark beard and his sailor's cap you can't help thinking about Captain Haddock from Tintin.

The leader doesn't like being looked at.

"Something's funny?" he asks.

"Not at all," says Jack.

"So would you mind telling me what you're looking for?"

Jack takes from his pocket the paper he wrote on before leaving.

"It's written on that."

"What's keeping you from reading it?" asks the leader, handing him the flashlight.

"It's pretty personal," says Jack. "There are too many people here."

"Okay you guys, give him some room."

"Thanks."

When everyone moves away in the direction of the big staircase he unfolds the paper and rereads it in the light from the flashlight. There are only three short sentences in which Jack assumes full responsibility for his act, but the wording now strikes him as feeble. Taking out his pen, he strikes out *before the total decline* and replaces it with *before the shipwreck*, the last word being more in keeping with the Québécois tradition of dipping into maritime terminology.

He hands the note back to Johnny. The gang-leader peruses it and declares without hesitation that he understands what Jack wants. However, he's not in agreement.

"It's too risky" he says. "I could spend the rest of my life inside... Why should I do that?"

"The dough!" says Jack.

Not only is his wallet well-stuffed, but he has on him as well a credit card and a cheque book. Shaken by these arguments, Johnny orders him not to move and goes to confer with the other gang members. When he comes back, he announces that he's changed his mind. Now he seems to be in a hurry.

"Are you ready?"

"Sure, but I'd prefer it to happen a little farther away, on the stairs."

"Why?"

"To be closer to the St. Lawrence and to have a better view of the lights of Lower Town and Lévis."

"Whatever you say. That gives me time to sort out the minor details."

He sends away the other members of the group except for one who seems to be his assistant. The two men flank old Jack and start down the stairs with him. The boss rubs the prints off the weapon. Then he grabs it by the barrel with a Kleenex and gives it back to Jack.

They go down another few steps.

"This is a good spot," says Jack. "The view is wonderful."

He lights one last cigarette, smokes half of it, then says that he's ready and presses the barrel of the pistol against his right temple. He keeps his gaze fixed on the lights shining on the other side of the river, waiting for the boss behind him to help pull the trigger... Instead of which he receives a violent blow to his skull and passes out.

When he comes back to himself dawn is breaking.

He manages to get to the bottom of the stairs, partly on his legs, partly on his elbows and knees. When he goes onto the long

Dufferin Terrace, his head is spinning and he has to lie down on a grassy slope. Later, an early-morning walker helps him get home. When he tries to give him a little money, he discovers that they've taken his wallet, his credit card, and his cheque book. On the other hand, he still has his pistol and the little note in the pocket of his windbreaker. And a seriously aching head.

On the rue du Rendez-Vous, my hot chocolate had got cold, the sky was totally black, and my heart felt as if it were caught in a vise. I thought about Jack. I thought about my little sister. I was afraid of losing them both. It was time to go home.

19

A Phony Sleazebag

Mistassini was waiting for me at the Quebec City airport. I had told her on the phone not to come, but she was there. She was standing very strangely, with her hands behind her back, and her shy smile was enticing. She was talking to me with her eyes and I was glad to see that nothing between us had changed. It was as if half of each of us was part of the other.

"Want to drive?" she asked, holding out the key. We were in the parking lot next to an old car — a Plymouth Duster from the 1980s. I stowed my suitcase in the trunk and kept my small knapsack with me.

"I'd rather you did," I said.

She got in, leaned across to open the door for me, and I got in beside her, wincing after the seven-hour flight.

"Who does this wonderful wreck belong to?"

"A friend."

Her answer gave me a twinge of sadness.

"It's all right," she said, "not a personal friend. A friend of Jack's."

She turned the key and when the engine was running, she pumped the gas pedal to show me that the car was in good shape despite its age. I acknowledged that the eight cylinders were purring softly but of course it was Jack I was thinking about.

As soon as the Duster started to move, something in the centre of me began to relax; up till then I hadn't even realized that my muscles were tense. I sensed that there was a kind of correspondence between what I really liked and all the details, beautiful or ugly, that made up the landscape. The vastness of the sky, the harshness of the light, the galleries of the houses, the fence pickets, the hydro wires, the spruce trees, even the white lines on the asphalt — everything suited me, everything told me that I was home.

"Is it okay if I go along Duplessis and then take chemin Saint-Louis?"

"Sure, but I'd like..."

"Yes, I know, I'll drive slowly."

She had her left elbow on the window frame and was holding the wheel with two fingers of her right hand. She slowed down on boulevard Duplessis to give me time to see everything, and she didn't speed up on chemin Saint-Louis, despite the line of cars behind us, so that I could greet the oak trees lining that old winding road. I stretched out my arm and stroked the very fine down on her neck, and she cocked her head to the right and rubbed her cheek against the back of my hand.

All was well, I was almost happy, but that well-being didn't last. Anxiety, which had been dormant since my arrival, stirred again just as we came to rue d'Auteuil.

"How is he?" I asked, because the question was burning my lips.

"Not too bad," she said.

I waited for an explanation. It didn't come so I thought that perhaps she didn't want to bombard me with worries right away. I thanked her with a smile, and while I went on looking around me I realized that contrary to the tourist guides, Vieux-Québec didn't have much in common with cities in France, the ones I'd visited anyway: the sidewalks, the outside staircases, the store windows, the number of storeys, the shutters, the colour of the stones and the roofs — nearly everything was different; Vieux-Québec resembled only itself and that was more than enough.

"You okay?" she asked softly, as if she were able to see things through my eyes.

"I'm just fine," I said.

"What would you like to do now?"

I looked at her from the corner of my eye to see if there was some intimation in her question. Most of the time there wasn't because Mist was perfectly guileless, but with my twisted mind I couldn't help checking. Just in case, I asked,

"What would you like?"

"No, you decide," she said.

"Okay. I assume he's at the store now?"

"Yes. He said you could rest up at his place. Is that okay with you? You could even have a nap if you want, then we'll come over and have supper with you tonight."

The offer was fine with me. I hadn't slept either in the plane, where my seat mate, a corpulent, talkative woman, had so to speak overflowed onto me, even entrusting her baby to me while she went to the bathroom, or the night before which I'd spent with Jack's Paris friends, with whom I left a few things, a message for the lovely Françoise and the keys to the Volks.

"Coming up?" I asked Mist when she'd parked the Duster across from Jack's place, on rue des Remparts. She shrugged. "Just for a minute!" I insisted plaintively. My heart would break into a thousand pieces unless she said yes right away, and the pieces would tumble down the Côte de la Canoterie and plunge into the St. Lawrence.

"All right, just for a minute," she said finally.

I took my big bag out of the car. She wanted to take it from me and carry it up to the apartment but I resisted, at the same time looking into her eyes, her blue eyes that were so luminous and transparent that I sometimes turned my head away so as not to look at them directly. Unlike her, I was far from guileless. During my rather tumultuous student days I'd even tried to become a real sleazebag; my attempts had failed and I'd realized that the excellent education I'd received from my family left me with no choice but to be a nice guy.

At Jack's place, just as I was depositing my bag by the sofa, all at once the fatigue of my trip swooped down on me.

"Do you want something to eat?" asked Mist. She was in the kitchen, I'd heard her open the fridge.

"Such as?"

"A piece of strawberry pie ... strawberries from the Île d'Orléans!"

"With vanilla ice cream?"

"Yes."

"I'd like that a lot, but first I have to shower because I ache all over!"

Hot water was the best way to completely relax all my muscles. I had in mind a statement by Epictetus: "As regards sexual matters, you should remain pure as far as you can ... and, if you indulge, let it be lawfully." I thought to myself that if I complained aloud about muscle spasms while I was in the shower, Mist might offer to massage my back. So I turned on the taps and started to moan loud enough to cover the sound of the water, stopping to listen for a reaction. I hadn't closed the bathroom door.

Finally, I heard Mist's voice.

"Coming!" she said. There were hurried footsteps and her voice, distant at first, came closer. "Can I come in?" she asked.

"Of course," I said, turning off both taps.

"Did you hurt yourself?"

"No. My muscles ache from the plane."

"Where?"

"Here!"

I pointed with my finger to my lumbar region or, more precisely, the top of my butt. She couldn't see anything of course, as the shower curtain was closed, but if everything proceeded as planned, she would open the curtain to see. Which she did, after asking permission. A kind of instinct which to my regret was more powerful than my lascivious ideas, compelled me to turn my back: that's the kind of thing I think about when I say that I'm not a true sleazebag.

She got into the shower with me and, placing both hands on my hips, began to massage me with her thumbs, tracing small circles, a muscle that Jack had named for me, that's called the piriformis. As Mist was a tennis player, she had a lot of strength in her fingers, and also tenderness and warmth. What she did felt very good, even if some pain was mixed with the pleasure when she pressed hard on a tense muscle. I could have let her do it all day long.

"That feels so good," I said, though I knew the remark was superfluous, as I'd been purring like a cat for five minutes.

"I'm glad," she said. "Anything else?"

"Yes..."

Without turning around, I placed my hands on top of hers. I spoke to her with gestures because the words that came to mind were intemperate: I mean that instead of being in harmony with feelings, words were always a note higher. I guided her hands and she let me. Afterwards, she began spontaneously to stroke my back. I wanted very much to turn around and I was on the verge of doing so, having summoned up all my courage, when she wrapped her arms around me and pressed herself against my back. She let her hands wander over my belly, at the same time rubbing her cheek against my shoulders. Now and then she would kiss my neck, producing a shudder that ran to the bottom of my spinal column.

If there was something unusual about our caresses, it may have been that they did not constitute a stage to cross so that we could go further. We could caress each other for a very long time without tiring and without wanting to move on to something else. That day, though, my little sister's mind was elsewhere.

"I have to get back to the store," she said, kissing my shoulder.

"I understand," I said.

"If I don't, he'll worry."

"You mean he's not doing well?"

She hesitated briefly.

"It's best not to leave him alone for too long," she said.

"I'll help you."

"All right, but first you're going to sleep for a while."

"Okay. Would you hand me the towel?"

She passed me Jack's big bath towel, the one with a reproduction of Hemingway's house in Key West. When she held it out to me I pretended to be daydreaming and as I'd hoped, she took the time to dry me off from head to toe. Except that the whole operation took no more than a minute for the simple reason that I was nearly dry when she started.

"See you tonight," she said. "Get some rest. The pie is on the table."

"Thanks, little sister."

Because of the jet lag, hot water, and cuddling, my brain had gone soft; my heart and all the rest, including my libido, weren't much better. I was moving as slowly as a sleepwalker.

I put on Jack's bathrobe and his sheepskin slippers, which were too big for me. Before tucking into my strawberry pie, I went into his library. Dictionaries were spread across his desk. I opened the *Petit Robert des noms propres*, and under *Hemingway, Ernest*, I read that the writer had blown his brains out just before he turned sixty-two. The age Jack was now.

In the kitchen the strawberry pie sat on the table with a scoop of vanilla ice cream, just as my little sister had told me. She'd put the pie in the oven for a moment to warm it slightly and to make the ice cream melt: she knew all my little idiosyncrasies. I'm always slightly chilly after a shower, so I opened the oven door to take advantage of the remaining warmth.

20

Jack and the Wonderful Lamp

Jack was summoned to the Hôtel-Dieu at ten o'clock Saturday morning. He didn't ask Mist or me for help, but he looked more and more distraught as the date approached, so I decided to go with him.

Across from us in the gerontology department waiting room there was a family consisting of an old man, a fortyish woman, and a little girl. The room was decorated with paintings of Charlevoix landscapes in autumn; on a corner table there was a pile of magazines as well as some books for children and a few toys.

The old man was sitting directly across from Jack. He gave off a smell of urine, faint but acrid, that made me uncomfortable. He was looking at Jack, apparently without seeing him, and my friend, as uncomfortable as I was, kept looking down.

The woman looked at her watch, then took a book from her bag. I recognized *The Crack-Up*, a collection of short stories by F. Scott Fitzgerald that Mist and I had read a while ago. The book had made a strong impression on us because of the writing, nimble and precise, which had a magical effect on us, a kind of fascination, like a neon sign spotted from a distance in the night. I stood up to get a magazine and as I walked past the woman, I saw that she was about halfway into the book. Another few pages and she would read the title essay, with its devastating first sentence that hit you like a punch in the belly: "Of course all life is a process of breaking down."

While I was wondering how the woman would react to that sentence, the little girl got down from her chair to pick up a colouring book. She looked about five or six, but I'm often wrong about that kind of thing. Her eyes were dark brown, nearly black, too big for her face. Her blonde hair was in pigtails adorned with multicoloured beads; she had on a flowered dress and white shoes.

Holding the colouring book she turned first to the grandfather. She opened her mouth as if to ask him a question, then changed her mind and looked at her mother. A moment later the woman looked up and in a gentle voice suggested that the child use the crayons on the table. Making a funny face, the little girl picked up the box of crayons, put it on a chair, and sat down, legs sticking out horizontally, on the one next to it.

My eyes went from mother to daughter. The mother, frowning, was reading very slowly, sometimes flipping back a few pages. The girl imitated her mother's anxious look and chose her colours carefully; I couldn't help smiling as I saw her colour an elephant blue, a tiger red, and a gazelle purple. She was starting to put green spots on a giraffe whose head emerged from a row of trees when for no apparent reason she stopped. She put the green crayon back in the box then went to her mother and showed her the animals.

The mother took a quick look at the drawing.

"That's very good," she assured the girl. "Blue elephants are the most beautiful elephants in the world."

"Yes," said the little girl, "but I wanted you to tell me the story."

"What story?"

She was back in Fitzgerald's book. She had got to the title story and I could see her eyes get bigger as she read the first sentence.

"The story about the elephant and the giraffe and how they get into the little house that's in the jungle and everything!"

"In a while. Mummy's busy."

The little girl tugged at her mother's arm to make her bend down and murmured something in her ear: I could make out the word "grandpa." She was talking not about her grandfather but about Jack, because the mother glanced in his direction.

"All right," said the mother, straightening up, "but only if you're nice to him and don't keep asking 'why' all the time."

"How many times?"

The mother held up three fingers on her left hand. The little girl sighed and nodded, then she went over to Jack with her open book. He had moved to the last chair at the back of the room and he was staring out the window.

"What are you looking at?" she asked.

"The sky," said Jack.

"Why?"

"Because it's beautiful."

"Is that where we go when we're too old?"

"Who said that?"

"Mummy."

"Then it must be true."

The little girl was whispering loudly and I had no trouble hearing what she said. She sat down next to Jack and asked, "Are you a grandpa too?"

"Of course I am," said Jack after a brief hesitation. "Doesn't it show?"

"My grandpa, we can't ask him to tell us stories."

"You can't?"

"No, because he forgot how."

"These things happen..."

Jack rolled his eyes and from his disappointed look I could tell that he wasn't happy with what he'd said and that he was thinking he was worthless.

"He forgot all kinds of things," said the little girl, still whispering loudly.

"Is that so?"

"Yes. He forgot how to eat by himself. Mummy feeds him with a spoon like me when I was little."

Jack made no comment. The little girl whispered something else, her voice fainter: I thought I could make out "grandpa" or "grandfather." Jack, who was a little hard of hearing, asked her to repeat it, and this time I had the clear impression, though I couldn't swear to it, that with an odd accent she was saying *Pampers*.

In the waiting room, no one seemed to attach any importance to what had just been said. The old man, slumped like an empty burlap bag, still wore an absent look. The mother was back in the world of Fitzgerald's blonde and fragile women. As for me, I didn't dare say a word and I was hoping that Jack wouldn't be demolished by the little girl's naivety. I was somewhat reassured when he asked,

"Did you want me to tell you a story?"

"Yes," she said, holding her book open at the page she'd just coloured.

"I can see what it is," he said, "but if you'll allow me I'd like to talk to the young man over there."

"Why?"

"To hold a consultation."

"What's a consultation?"

"It's when people get together to tell a story."

With a curved finger, the little girl beckoned me to join them. I sat down beside her. Jack, sitting on the other side, placed the book on his knees and I leaned over to look at the drawings.

"I can see what the story is," I declared in turn. "It's the story of Noah's Ark. Do you know the story of our grandfather Noah and his Ark?"

"Of course I know it! I'm not a baby!" she exclaimed. And by way of proof, she started to sing a song that begins, "Our grandfather Noah, a worthy patriarch." She sang a few verses, still whispering, and I refrained from telling her that she sometimes confused the words with another song about a little ship that was taking "a long journey across the Med-Med-Mediterranean." When she'd finished I started to tell a story.

"For a long, long time, Noah's Ark had been sailing across the sea. There was hardly any wind so it wasn't going very far. Now the rain had stopped and the animals didn't have anything to drink or eat. Grandfather Noah had asked the elephants to pump up some sea water with their trunks, and since the water in the Mediterranean is blue, they turned all blue themselves!"

The little girl burst into laughter that rang out loud and clear, even though she'd put both her hands in front of her mouth. Her laughter was still echoing off the walls and in the corridor when a nurse arrived. She led the old man away and the mother followed, asking us to keep an eye on her daughter for a few minutes. She was carrying a suitcase that she'd taken from under the table in the corner, where it had been hidden among the biggest toys.

I opened wide the window to get rid of the smell that still floated in the room.

Around fifteen minutes later, the woman came back, alone and red-eyed. Nevertheless she gave her daughter a little smile when the girl refused to go.

"The story isn't over!" she protested.

Jack and I, taking over from one another, had embarked on a silly story. Noah's Ark had landed at a mysterious island whose natives, when they spotted the animals, had abandoned their huts to hide in the forest. When the deluge started up again, the animals sought refuge in the empty huts and we'd drawn happy giggles from the little girl when we told her how the giraffe stuck his head out a chimney so he could graze on the high branches of trees, which made his spots turn green.

While we were racking our brains to come up with a plausible explanation for the red colour of the tiger, the nurse came out to get Jack. There was such distress in my old friend's eyes that I decided to go with him. I said goodbye to the little girl and her mother, and the nurse showed us to an examining room with a dressing room next to it. She showed Jack into the dressing room, asking me to wait in the corridor. Reluctantly, I obeyed, but a glance inside the examining room showed me that it didn't contain anything disquieting: a table that could be adjusted to various positions, an ultrasound device with a number of screens, and a second, smaller device inscribed with the word Uroflowmetry that indicated he'd be undergoing an examination of his urinary system.

Leaving the room a good hour later, Jack confirmed that he had had that examination, as well as blood tests and an X-ray of his spine. They were normal checks, in my opinion, taking his age into account. When I asked him for details though, he grabbed my arm and led me to the stairs, glancing furtively around him. And outside, while we were walking quickly towards his apartment, he told me that instead of examinations, he'd undergone a memory test that required him to remember a series of numbers that grew longer and longer, and a personality test that required him to make a number of drawings, including a landscape, a tree, and a self-portrait.

In his opinion, those examinations were intended to determine whether he was still productive. He had the impression that he'd made a mess of them all. To get revenge on the gerontologist, at the end of the interview he had deliberately made some disconcerting remarks. He'd said that he wanted to be cremated, and when the doctor asked him why, he'd replied that the urn that held his ashes would no doubt be stored in some closet and sit there, forgotten, for years ... But one fine day a very poor cleaning lady would find it and she would quite naturally rub the dust off it and then, as in the story of "Aladdin's Lamp," he would emerge from the urn in the form of a genie who was well disposed to grant some of her wishes, even the most extravagant ones.

21

A Ghost

We had to face facts: Jack had only intermittent contact with reality and at any moment that contact was liable to blow like a fuse and Mist and I had not yet learned how to recognize the warning signs of a breakdown.

Already there had been an incident during a party Jack had given the day after my return. It was held at the bookstore. Because he detested stars, media-conscious writers, and people desperate for fame, Jack had invited the usual customers and some street people from Place d'Youville. Among them was the thin grey-haired woman he'd met in a restaurant on rue d'Auteuil one night just before he was attacked on the big staircase of Dufferin Terrace.

We'd lit a fire in the stove, but only for the aroma and the crackling wood; it wasn't cold. With the wine and beer there was atmosphere and even a bit of a hullabaloo for the greater pleasure of everyone except Charabia, who had left the desk drawer and perched on the highest shelf. I was supposed to be the centre of interest but happily all eyes were on Mist: she'd put on her blue Québec Nordiques T-shirt that emphasized her sharp bones and her little curves.

Like everyone else, the thin woman was distracted by the T-shirt. She'd had a lot of wine and beer and you could see that she was struggling to remember something.

"I've got a book in my head!" she declared abruptly.

"What kind of book?" asked Mist.

All three of us — Jack, Mist, and me — were standing around her. The situation wasn't new. How many times had people asked for a book of which they'd forgotten the title and author and could only provide us with vague clues, such as its size or colour? Satisfying readers like that is one of the hardest parts of the bookseller's profession.

"A book with a bunch of separate stories," she explained. "And in one of the stories there's a woman who gets lost when she's driving down a country road in the middle of nowhere and she can make out some blue hills... Wait a minute, it's coming back: 'A chain of blue hills, half-transparent.' That I remember because way back when, I learned it by heart. But now, I've forgotten the title..."

It was at that moment that the incident occurred. According to Jack, it was a phrase from his last book. Mist hadn't dared contradict him but at the end of the evening, when we started cleaning up and he'd gone to the Parenthesis to pour some milk for Charabia, she showed me that it was from a book by Gabrielle Roy, *The Road Past Altamont*. It was the second time he'd made this kind of mistake.

A few weeks later there was a new alert. It was evening and I was alone in the store with the cat: Mist had taken old Jack home and wasn't back yet. It was past eleven o'clock. She never told me when she was coming back and sometimes she didn't come back at all, but this time I was tormented by doubt and worry. Unable to read or work, I paced, stopping at the store window to crane my neck and see if she was outside, close by, walking back along rue Saint-Jean. A fine rain, driven by the wind, was slanting down.

When the phone rang I knew right away that something had happened. It was Mist. She was still at Jack's and asked me to come. From her tone of voice I knew that it was urgent. As quickly as I could, I gave Charabia enough kibble and milk for two days and after I'd stowed in a plastic bag my tooth brush and Mist's and the two T-shirts we used as pyjamas, I was about to rush outside when an idea stopped me dead. It was mean and I wasn't proud of myself, but I didn't have time to weigh the pros and cons: going back to the Parenthesis, I hung Mist's T-shirt on the doorknob where she kept it, as if I'd forgotten it, and raced outside. I sped down rue Saint-Jean, then I took rue Couillard and rue de l'Université, which went straight to Jack's apartment. The wind had chased the clouds away and I could see that the moon was nearly full.

Mist was waiting for me on the landing to which the first steps led. She said hi and didn't add anything else. I couldn't read her eyes, which were nearly closed from fatigue, so I gave her a questioning look. She murmured a few snatches of sentences: Jack's fuse had blown, it was serious but not tragic, it might be enough to stay with him till he'd recovered.

Even though it was late, Jack was working in the library. As was his habit he was standing, or rather half-standing and half-sitting, his back resting against a chest of drawers surmounted by a small shelf unit, and his elbows were resting on the red plastic crate that he'd set up on his work table. His notebook was on the crate in front of him. He was holding a pen and staring into space. When he saw me he shook his head.

"I haven't finished my translation," he said sadly.

"It doesn't matter," I said.

"I'd promised it to the publisher before winter..."

"You've got plenty of time: there hasn't been a speck of snow!"

"But the publisher was here! Didn't you run into him when you arrived?"

"No."

"That means he went to Gabrielle's place."

"Right, you have the same publisher..."

When I took a seat next to Mist on a sofa, she gave me a look like a mother hen, though it wasn't at all her style; her style was independent, free, something like that. She wanted to thank me for finding the right tone to use with Jack and her look was as warm as a woollen scarf.

The silence persisted. Just for something to say I turned towards Jack and remarked, "You're working late tonight."

"I have to," he said. "For a few weeks now I've been having more and more trouble finding the right words. They come drop by drop. I have the impression that I'm a dried-up well, but I'm not allowed to give up: coming up with the right words is a courtesy to the reader... Is there a light on down there, on the other side of the terrace?"

Mist got up and went to the kitchen where the French door opened onto the terrace and onto the two steps that led to the mysterious chamber.

"No, there's no light on," she said when she came back.

"So they left together. They saw that I was working and didn't want to disturb me. That was nice of them."

"Would you prefer it if we let you work now?"

"No, I'm stopping. I'll call it a day, as my friend in Key West used to say when I spent the winter in that part of the world. Would you be able to translate that sentence?"

He was addressing me. I knew the translation but I pretended to rack my brains for a minute or two.

"I know," I said finally. "*Ça suffit pour aujourd'hui.*"

"Very good!" he said in English. "But in Key West, since it was nearly always sunny and warm, it was no later than noon when my friend made that remark. After that we'd go fishing."

"What kind of fishing?" I asked, a little worried.

"Deep sea fishing. First we'd go to his place, the big house with a brick wall around it and overrun with cats. We'd get the fishing gear and the sandwiches ready, then we'd take off for the Gulf Stream in his boat, his boat that was called..."

Hands together in front of his face, elbows resting on his plastic crate, he searched his memory as hard as he could, but the name of the boat was lost in the fog that enveloped the warm water of the Florida strait somewhere between Key West and Cuba. For a long moment he kept trying, but in vain.

"I can't remember," he said.

"It doesn't matter," said Mist. I could tell from the sad look on her face, and because I nearly always can read her thoughts, that she knew the name of the boat as well as I did and that she preferred to be silent so as not to humiliate old Jack.

"My memory's full of holes," he said. "Besides that, I don't feel very well: I'm old on the outside and young on the inside, and tonight the gap between the two is like a crevice."

His remarks were pessimistic, but the tone was that of a simple observation. It was a sign that he was gradually resuming contact with reality. While he rambled again a couple of times at the end of the evening, it was only when talking about Gabrielle, and on that subject we were used to his language confusion.

As a precaution though we decided to spend the night. Despite his fatigue, Jack wasn't sleepy. He played some songs from the past, the ones he played with the aim of exercising his memory, then he started to wander through the apartment, going from the bedroom to the living room, which overlooked the St. Lawrence, and stopping at the French door in the kitchen to glance anxiously at the room on the other side of the terrace.

Of late, Mist had been expending a lot of energy and among our customers there was now a whole network of people who knew Jack's songs by heart. At the slightest sign of amnesia he could call on one of them: they would sing him the lyrics without making a mistake and he was comforted as much by the warmth of their voices as by their memory. The cashier at the Richelieu had learned "Quand les hommes vivront d'amour," by Raymond Lévesque; the nurse at the Hôtel-Dieu knew "La Complainte de la Butte," which talked about Montmartre, the rue Saint-Vincent, staircases that were too steep, and windmills that protected lovers; Mist specialized in "Le Petit Bonheur," by Félix Leclerc; and I could sing "La Chanson de Prévert" by Serge Gainsbourg, who had put all the melancholy in his soul into the phrase, "day after day our dead loves die again and again." And Jack, no doubt in tribute to Ray Bradbury, enjoyed referring to each member of the network by the title of the song he'd learned.

Since he had played them so often, Mist and I knew most of Jack's songs by heart. We sang them with him that night. When he put on the song by Raymond Lévesque, I let my sister sing alone with him. Her voice was so limpid, so incredibly pure that I forgot to breathe while I was listening. Her eyes got blurry when she came to the words, "but as for us, my brother, we'll be dead," and I knew that she was thinking about the "little push" that Jack had talked about with me.

After that, Jack put on one of Léo Ferré's first records, the one with nothing but poems by Aragon. As I was helping him remember the words, Mist gestured to me that she was going to take a shower and my heart began to race. She rummaged in my plastic bag, took out her toothbrush and then, as she couldn't find her T-shirt in the colours of the former Nordiques, she took mine without a moment's hesitation. As she walked past me she gave me an angry look. I was expecting an outburst, but she'd done it for a laugh: she put her arms around my neck and rubbed her nose against mine. Her mocking eyes said that she wasn't cross with me.

For the rest of the evening I behaved myself and tried to make myself invisible. I let her make the decisions about where and when we'd sleep. I took a shower and to replace my T-shirt, borrowed a sweater of Jack's that came almost down to my knees, then I helped my sister turn the sofa in the library into a double bed. Jack was calmer now, he yawned and his eyes began to close. To wish my sister goodnight he put his arms around her and held her tightly against him, with one hand on the middle of her back and the other at the top of her little bum. Since she's even thinner than I am, she was bent backwards, like a bow held tense by a bowstring, and there wasn't one centimetre of her that wasn't pressed against him. I wasn't jealous though, I swear I wasn't jealous.

Jack gathered up what he needed for the night: book, alarm clock, flashlight, pills, mineral water, radio. Before he got into bed he lit a cigarette and put on one last record: the "Chanson pour l'Auvergnat" by Brassens. He particularly liked the verse that said:

It was only a spoonful of honey
But it warmed my body
And burns even now in my soul
Like the huge ball of the sun.

And, when the singer repeated for the last time, "May it take you across heaven to our eternal Father," Jack left the room and went to bed, looking rather serene. Mist went with him, whispered something, but didn't go inside, and he shut the door. She came back to the entrance to the library and stopped, her finger on the light switch. Sitting on the bed that we'd just made together, I waited for her to switch off the light before I pulled off the sweater that was all I had on. In her eyes, mocking as they'd been before, I thought I could see something that was as sweet to me as the honey in Brassens' song. She had no intention of switching off the light: she was challenging me. First I pretended that I didn't know what look to assume, then I got up and took off the sweater, with slowed-down movements, as in a movie, and I folded it carefully before setting it down on a chair. She said nothing, didn't make a move, but her eyes were locked with mine while, struggling to hold onto a minimum of dignity, I slowly got into the bed and slipped between the sheets.

I was torn between pleasure and fear: little sleazebags of my ilk like things that are somewhat equivocal, such as confused feelings, the line between dog and wolf.

She switched off the light and got in with me.

In the middle of the night she moved in her sleep, waking me. We were back to back. All at once she turned around and snuggled up to me: she may have been having a nightmare. Instead of staying motionless as usual, I put one arm behind her and, half turning onto my back, I tried to pull her towards me so that she'd throw her knee across my legs, with her elbow on my stomach, and her head on my shoulder: I wanted to feel her even closer to me. I'd almost achieved my goal when suddenly she woke up. But it wasn't my movement that had wakened her: she'd heard something.

"What's that?" she said, opening her eyes.

"No idea," I said.

"Didn't you hear a strange sound?"

"No, I was asleep," said the biggest liar in Vieux-Québec.

She sat up and leaned across to turn on a lamp. Separated from her now, I suddenly shivered, yet the night wasn't really cold, only cool and a little damp.

"Wait, I hear something again," she said.

"So do I," I said.

"It sounds like the kitchen door..."

She got up quickly, her T-shirt hiked up on her slender legs. I pulled on my sweater and followed her. The patio door in the kitchen, open onto the terrace, was ajar and moving back and forth in the wind. Mist went to close it, then her gaze froze. Stepping closer, I saw a ghost in the middle of the terrace: Jack, of course, but he was wrapped in a bedsheet that covered him completely, including his head. His arms were stretched out on either side of him and with the sheet flapping in the wind, you'd have said that he was going to take flight.

"Do you think it's a relapse?" I asked.

"I've no idea," she said, "but, whatever it is, he's liable to catch cold."

"I'll bring him in."

"No, let me."

It was the best thing to do. With luck, he would take her for Gabrielle and obey her, assuming he was having another problem with a fuse. While I held the door open, she went out onto the terrace. She stood between him and the railing, with her back to it. This was no time to be romantic, but I couldn't help thinking that the silhouette of my little sister, picked out by the milky light of the full moon, with the T-shirt that the wind plastered against her legs, had something attractive and very moving about it.

Almost at once, she turned towards him. She approached, touched his hand, and from the way he let himself be guided, smiling slightly, towards the kitchen and then the bedroom where the door closed behind them, I realized that the crisis had passed and that nothing serious was going to happen tonight.

I slept all alone for the rest of the night.

In the morning, I was the one who got up early to open the bookstore. Mist arrived much later. I didn't ask any questions, that's not my style.

22

A Carpet of Light

Mist and I were a little zouave, a little loony. We didn't follow the same rules as everybody else and for us that was something to be proud of. It didn't stop us from watching out for Jack's well-being day and night; we even tried to predict how things were going to develop in his case. It was with that notion in mind that I paid a visit to the gerontologist at the Hôtel-Dieu.

The specialist saw me right away. The walls of his office were decorated with children's drawings, but I didn't dare ask why.

"Are you a relative of Mr Waterman's?" he asked.

"Of course," I said, long convinced that we have permission to lie if it will avert pointless explanations.

"We don't see much of you..."

"I've been in France. How is he?"

He tapped on his computer keyboard. As he got no response, he grew impatient and went to get a file from a metal cabinet. All at once he started to laugh.

"I remember," he said. "He'd been hit on the head. I suggested an MRI, but he said it would be pointless because the blow had put his ideas back where they belonged. He said that he felt better than before!"

"So what did you do?"

"I insisted. The funny thing is, he was right: the MRI was better than the ones he'd had before! Several blood vessels were apparently no longer blocked..."

"How do you explain that?"

He shrugged. With his round, orangey-brown glasses, he resembled a short-eared owl, and his eyes, enlarged by the thick lenses, seemed to say that life was an inexhaustible source of surprises.

"I can't explain it."

"In the future, what should we be ready for?"

"I have no idea. As you can see, I don't know much."

"Do you at least know if he really is suffering from ... from what he calls Eisenhower's disease?"

Jack's file was thin. The specialist was engrossed for a moment in reading some reports, then he examined a few negatives in the light of his desk lamp.

"Does he have blackouts?"

"Sometimes," I said.

"He loses his sense of direction?"

"Sometimes he looks a little lost..."

"Does he see or hear things that other people don't?"

It was my turn to be perplexed: hadn't the doctor just set out the role of the writer? As a precaution, I was careful not to mention the fact that Jack sometimes caught sight of Gabrielle's silhouette in the top-floor window when he came home on nights when the moon was full.

The interview wasn't proceeding the way I'd hoped. To my questions, the gerontologist replied most often with other questions, and I realized after fifteen minutes that he wasn't sure of anything, that he was waiting to see how things would develop.

Leaving the hospital, I stopped at the Richelieu to pick up a frozen dinner of salmon with sorrel and rice. It was a recipe for two, very easy to fix on the little hotplate: you just had to heat the packages in boiling water. If Jack felt like joining us, we could always add another portion of rice.

When I walked into the bookstore at half-past five, Jack was there. I was glad that I was carrying a bag of groceries: he could see that I'd been shopping so he wouldn't suspect that I was coming from the Hôtel-Dieu. He and Mist were leaning on the counter, shoulder to shoulder, and doing the day's finances. He could have been her grandfather.

Jack wanted to go home for supper by himself because he had "some things to write." Mist walked him home and while I waited for her I found another book on the counter: *The Old Man and the Sea*. Along with the collection of short stories I'd received in Paris, this was the fourth book that Jack had left out for me. And since I was getting to know Hemingway's books quite well, I had no trouble understanding why this novel had been put out: it had the same qualities as the three previous ones, and it was universal as well, because it dealt with the search for happiness.

Mist came back later than expected. I played at being the translator deep in his dictionaries who doesn't even hear the front door open: I jumped when I noticed her all at once, and my phony look of surprise made her smile.

"Sorry to be so late," she said.

"Is everything all right?" I asked.

"Yes, it's fine."

"Was Gabrielle there?"

"No, not this time. Are you hungry?"

"Famished!"

In the Parenthesis I put water to boil on the hotplate and in a few minutes supper was ready. It was neither good nor bad: the frozen salmon didn't have much taste and the sorrel sauce was too rich, but food wasn't terribly important to us, it was just an opportunity to be together. In any case, Charabia always cleaned our plates.

I told Mist about my visit to the Hôtel-Dieu gerontologist, then she related Jack's latest remarks. He'd told her that morning: "It's not me that you see, it's my father. But I'm hidden inside that image: you can't see me." Having put everything together and weighed it carefully, we concluded that anything at all might happen and that it was best not to leave him alone for too long.

She suggested, "I could sleep there tonight..."

"As you wish," I said, trying desperately to make her understand without saying it that my heart would be not so heavy if she'd be good enough not to leave too soon. She looked at me and I didn't need to talk.

"Let's go out and walk for a while."

"I love you very much," I said very softly.

She did not reply. After we'd opened the window in the little room for Charabia, we stepped out onto rue Saint-Jean. The air was bracing, the days shorter, skirts longer, and, as always in autumn, a hint of foreboding shone in the eyes of old people and cats.

Vieux-Québec is not very big and nearly everyone knows one another, but no one could see that I was holding my little sister's hand as we walked because I kept it in my windbreaker pocket; her hand was warm and smooth and there was no limit to the very simple pleasure it gave me to lace my fingers with hers.

To be sure that Mist didn't go directly to Jack's place after our walk, I led her in the opposite direction to rue des Remparts, towards the west. I took her across Place d'Youville and the gloomy boulevard Dufferin, then we stepped into the neighbourhood of Saint-Jean-Baptiste. The area lacked trees and green spaces, but to compensate and to rest our eyes when we were strolling the terraced streets on the slope that led to the Lower Town, at every intersection we were able to admire the vast carpet of light that spread as night was falling from Limoilou to the feet of the Laurentians.

We were at the corner of de La Tourelle and Sainte-Marie. I squeezed my little sister's hand more tightly.

"The expression that comes to mind is *carpet of light*," I said, shaking my head. "Can you imagine?"

"You mean it's a cliché?"

"Yes. But that's not what is bothering me most."

"What's bothering you?"

It was hard to explain and I wasn't sure myself that there was anything honest about what I wanted to say.

"Look," I said. "For some time now, whenever I see something out of the ordinary I've been spending hours looking for the words to describe it with the greatest precision. I'm very afraid that I belong to the race of lunatics who prefer words to things."

"Like Jack?"

"Yes."

We went home along the edge of the cliff so that we wouldn't miss a moment of the show. Mist had more imagination than I did, the lights in the night made her think about movie stars in tuxedos, evening gowns, and rivers of diamonds, who stood in the shadows at the Oscars.

The Côte d'Abraham brought us to rue Saint-Jean and the bookstore. Mist agreed to stop for a hot chocolate. Young Charabia hadn't come back, but, from the smell in the Parenthesis and the fact that the bowl of kibble was empty, we could tell that some of his friends had dropped in.

I set the steaming cups on the counter. It was just after ten. To avoid attracting attention, we'd only switched on the nightlight in the Parenthesis, leaving us in the half-light. I put a little piece of birch in the stove, just enough to make it flare: that was a trick to keep Mist there longer because she liked to hear the crackling of a fire.

"Remember?" she asked.

"What?"

"The old fieldstone fireplace."

"Oh yes, I remember it very well."

She took little sips of her chocolate and wrapped her arm around my shoulders. We had a shared memory of which there only remained two or three images that had fallen like autumn leaves deep into our souls. We were in a chalet that my father had built on the bank of the river. Even though we were very young, too young to go to the village school, we had helped him pick up stones along the roadside to build a fireplace in the chalet. One afternoon, confined to the cottage by a cold November rain, Mist and I had got under the covers in front of the fireplace. That was how we discovered in total innocence and a with fit of giggling that we weren't absolutely alike, and we had held onto a memory filled with wonder that had united us ever since.

"Drink while it's hot," she said.

I took a sip, then I slipped my hand inside her sweatshirt where there was lots of room since she had nothing on under it. Her head moved little by little until it settled on my shoulder, and the crackling of the fire was soon joined by a kind of purring. After a moment that seemed to me very brief, she raised her head and looked at the time on her watch. Then she brought her face close to mine and blew on my eyes to make me close them and then, very delicately, with the tip of her tongue, she traced the outline of my lips. It was the first time she'd done this, I felt paralyzed and my heart was pounding as I let her go on.

She put a few things in a knapsack and I waved to her from the front window. There was no end to her surprises: her rejection of the norms and of accepted ideas was stronger than mine. As for me, I spent my time imagining embraces and bold caresses, but that was when she wasn't there. When she was there I was intimidated, content to murmur things to her, to brush her cheek or her back, and sometimes, at night, to press myself against her while pretending to be asleep.

23

The Writer

One night the phone rang and it took me a few seconds to realize that I wasn't dreaming. It was the phone in the bookstore. Anxious, I got up, put on my slippers, and hurried to the desk in the store.

"Hello?"

"It's Mistassini!"

"Hi little sister! What's up?"

I turned my head to look at the Indian crafts boutique located diagonally across the street: the big luminous clock on the back wall showed three a.m.

"Jack's had a relapse and I've tried everything..."

"Is it serious?"

"He's talking about the *little push*..."

"I'll be right there!"

Charabia couldn't comprehend my behaviour and wouldn't get out of the bed even when I gave him a piece of leftover chicken. He looked on, bewildered, while I dressed in what I'd worn the day before. Over my T-shirt I put on the black sweater that Mist had knit for me and flew out of the bookstore. I ran the whole way, stopping for not much more than thirty seconds at the corner of Sainte-Famille and de l'Université to urinate into a manhole; the air wasn't too cold, it might be Indian Summer.

Climbing up the stairs to the apartment on rue des Remparts, I expected cries or raised voices, but there was no sound at all. Inside it was almost totally dark: all I saw was a faint light coming from the bedroom.

First I visited the other rooms, tiptoeing, afraid of I don't know what macabre discovery. Everything was normal in the living room and kitchen and there weren't any ghosts on the terrace. Somewhat reassured, I crossed the library and before going into the bedroom, I started making a little noise to announce my presence; I coughed a few times and kicked a chair, swearing as if I'd just tripped. Then, as the door was ajar, I went in without knocking.

They were in the big bed. Old Jack, lying on his back, was holding Mist in his arms; she lay on her side with her head on his shoulder. But he wasn't holding her in the usual way: he was clinging to her as if he were afraid. He was pale and his eyes were bulging. The Beretta was on the bedside table.

The sight of the pistol had me rooted to the spot. I couldn't react and that helplessness exasperated me: a true sleazebag wouldn't let something like that impress him. It took me a while to pull myself together.

"Who wants coffee?" I asked in a tiny voice.

No one answered. My voice must have been even fainter than I thought. Then I heard, "Me!"

It was Mist. She'd given a very good imitation of my quavery voice and Jack himself, despite his suffering, couldn't help smiling and loosening his arms. She could have freed herself and got out of the bed, but she didn't budge: she was perfect.

In the kitchen, I lit the fire under the kettle and tried to think. The moment I'd been fearing since the beginning had arrived and I realized that far from being ready for it I had done all I could, in both Paris and Quebec, to forget it. I'd even cherished the hope that Jack would abandon his plan. Now the time had come: he was going to talk about that *little push*. I'd lacked the courage to refuse in the beginning when he'd asked for my help, and now I had to assume the consequences of my cowardice.

While the water was heating up, I'd racked my brains trying to think what to do, but nothing came. Looking around me, I noticed one detail that I hadn't bothered with when I came in: on the table and on the fridge there were notes written by Mist to remind Jack of certain things that he tended to forget, such as the phone numbers of friends, or where he kept the keys to the apartment. When I opened the cupboard to take out the tin of coffee, I spotted another note, written by Jack, that quoted the following remarks by Epictetus: "The festival is over. Leave it and depart like a grateful and modest person; make room for others. Others too must be born, as you were, and when they are born must have land and houses and the necessities of life. But if those who come first do not withdraw, what room is there left? Why are you insatiable? Why are you never satisfied? Why do you crowd the world?"

"Coffee's ready!" I announced, trying to make my voice firmer.

I didn't expect a reply but in they came, holding each other's hand; Mist was pulling on Jack's, but you could hardly see it. They sat at the table, started to drink, and I noted that Jack's face had changed:

after his crises, his look of terror always gave way to a melancholy expression.

He looked at the clock on the stove.

"It's very late," he said, turning towards me. "Sorry, but it's the moment we talked about."

I hung my head without saying a word, wanting only not to give the impression that I approved of his plan. Holding my cup in both hands, I took a few sips. Instead of the original idea, which I still hoped would get me out of the impasse, all that came to me were fragments of images: my sister leaving the house, my father's rifle killing the old sick dog with one shot, my mother learning that she had cancer...

Jack was watching me.

"You want an explanation?" he asked wearily.

"No. I don't want anything at all," I said.

"All the same I'm going to try."

He downed his coffee then looked at his cup, surprised, as if someone else had emptied it. Mist got up and refilled it. It was real coffee, an expert blend of mocha and java that was very good.

"All right," he said. "Certain things are hard to bear, things that I don't like at all. I don't like the creases in my skin, my wobbly legs, my yellow teeth, my bad breath, my limp dick, my falling hair, my runny nose, my memory that lets me down, my trembling heart, and the fear of the unknown that's sweeping over me..."

He interrupted himself. Mist's face, and no doubt mine as well, was growing longer along with his list of complaints. He realized that he'd laid it on a little too thick, then added,

"Basically I could accept all that for a while if I were writing something; I mean something important and original. I get all kinds of ideas but I don't like them: there's an air of déjà vu about them.

If this goes on I'm going to become an old writer. Eisenhower's Disease stops me from having new ideas."

"What is an old writer?" I asked naively.

"A writer who only looks behind him."

"Can't we help you?" asked Mist.

I saw a half-smile on Jack's face. He was starting to relax.

"That's sweet of you," he said, "but first I'd have to get younger! Obviously if someone were to take my place..."

He stole a glance at me. I was on my guard. In a voice that was practically cheerful, he went on.

"Someone younger... Someone who would have learned the trade by doing translations and who consequently would write soberly, without the tendency to be lyrical that I hate... Someone who would have done some travelling to knock some sense into him..."

"I know that you're thinking about me," I said. "And I've seen the books you've put out for me... They're like Hansel and Gretel's white pebbles, right?"

He looked away, seeming embarrassed.

"As for the travelling," I added, "there's something I have to confess... In France last summer, I hardly moved; I only left Paris two or three times, to see car races: the 24 Hours of Le Mans, the Grand Prix de France..."

"I've nothing against car races!" he said.

"Wait... I could never write!"

And then I launched into the list of the weaknesses that nature had inflicted on me.

"Don't worry," he said. "We do our best writing from our weaknesses."

I insisted on the volatility of my nature, the poverty of my imagination, and I added everything else that came into my head.

Needless to say, it was the little sleazebag who was talking. I hadn't taken the time to understand that Jack's proposal was the only way to avoid the tragic ending we were being swept towards at full speed. It was an opportunity not to be missed, but I couldn't decently recognize it at first. So I pretended to hesitate, to be weighing the pros and cons.

"Who'll look after the bookstore?" I asked.

"I will," said Mistassini. "I've got a few ideas for making people feel totally at home."

"Where will I go to write?"

"You'll come here," said Jack. "In good weather you'll go out on the little terrace, facing the river: the view goes on forever and when you're starting out it's good for inspiration. I'll teach you the tricks that Hemingway used. I'll show you how, if you want to get a story started, you just have to write the truest sentence that you know; how you must endeavour to write only about the things you know best; how you have to leave a sentence suspended at the end of your day to give you momentum when you start to work the next day."

He fell silent abruptly and indicated by spreading his hands that he had more to say but that he was tired. I could see some anxiety in Mist's eyes.

"Okay, I'll give it a try," I said.

"Maybe you'd rather take a few days to think it over?"

"No, I've decided."

I wanted to appear as firm as possible. In my mind though I wasn't really making a commitment. I intended to make an honest effort over several months, hoping that everything would go well. And, if the experiment didn't work out, I'd go back to translation and it wouldn't be the end of the world. Maybe in the meantime old Jack would have regained his ability to write something new, to get a kind of second wind.

"Gabrielle will help you too," said Jack.

"Of course," I said.

I glanced at Mist. She moved her head to tell me to look at the clock on the stove, then she smiled at me very sweetly. It meant that the question of the *little push* had been taken care of for the moment, that Jack was tired and was liable to have a fuse problem, that she was going to give him his pills and help him get to sleep, and that I could now go back to the bookstore.

On my way there I took a detour to help me think straight. Because there was a nip in the air, Mist lent me Jack's windbreaker to put on over my black sweater. I went down the Côte de la Canoterie and walked for a while along the docks in the Bassin Louise. Behind the old grain silos, beyond the Île d'Orléans and the south shore of the St. Lawrence, a pale light on the horizon was getting bigger, extinguishing the stars one by one.

There was no one out and I couldn't hear a thing, not even a gull. It was the moment of silence that precedes the dawn. With this day, a new life was beginning for me and I was amazed not to feel any different.

Once I was back at the bookstore I realized that wasn't so. Lying on the bottom bunk with Charabia, I was waiting for Mist to return while the day was breaking; I was impatient, I could feel the venom of jealousy creeping into my veins when all at once it occurred to me that from now on, I wouldn't be really unhappy because I would always be able to put the things that made me sad into a story and attribute them to a character.

Comforted by that thought, I fell asleep.